# The hunters Guide to Monsters

# EB Robichaud

# Table of Contents

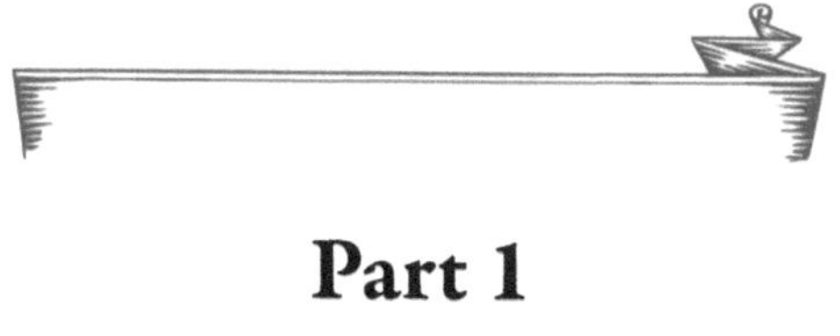

# Part 1

# Werewolves

# Werewolves

## 1.

Werewolves have been a part of popular culture for centuries, and their influence can be seen in literature, film, television, and even video games. The idea of a werewolf has been around since ancient times, and the concept of a human transforming into a wolf has been a part of folklore and mythology for centuries.

The concept of a werewolf has been a part of popular culture since the Middle Ages, when it was believed that certain individuals were possessed by a wolf spirit and could transform into a wolf. This belief was so pervasive that werewolves were hunted and killed in some parts of Europe. In the late 19th century, the horror genre began to take shape, and werewolves were one of the first monsters to be featured in literature and film.

The most iconic werewolf in popular culture is undoubtedly the character of the Wolfman, first introduced in the 1941 film The Wolf Man. The Wolfman was portrayed by Lon Chaney Jr., and his portrayal of the character has become the standard for werewolves in popular culture. The Wolfman was a tragic figure, cursed to transform into a wolf on the night of a full moon. He was a sympathetic character, and the audience was able to empathize with his plight.

The Wolfman has been featured in numerous films, and the character has been adapted in various ways. In some films, the Wolfman is a villain, while in others he is a hero. The Wolfman has also been featured in television shows and video games, and his popularity has endured for decades.

Werewolves have also been featured in other forms of popular culture, including comic books and novels. The character of the Werewolf of London, first introduced in the 1930s, is a classic example of a werewolf in literature. In comic books, the character of Wolfsbane is a popular werewolf character, and she has been featured in various X-Men stories.

The popularity of werewolves has endured for centuries, and their influence can be seen in various forms of popular culture. Werewolves are often used as a metaphor for the darker aspects of human nature, and their stories are often used to explore themes of fear, transformation, and the battle between good and evil. Werewolves have been a part of popular culture for centuries, and their influence can be seen in literature, film, television, and even video games.

2.

Killing a werewolf is no easy task, and it can be a dangerous endeavor. It is important to understand that werewolves are not just mythical creatures, but they are actually real and can be found in certain parts of the world. As such, it is important to take the proper precautions when attempting to kill a werewolf.

The first step to killing a werewolf is to understand their weaknesses. Werewolves have several weaknesses that can be exploited, such as silver, wolfsbane, and holy water. Silver is the most effective weapon against a werewolf, as it can penetrate their thick hide and cause them pain. Wolfsbane is also effective, as it can cause the werewolf to become weakened and disoriented. Holy water is also effective, as it can cause the werewolf to become sick and weak.

Once you have determined the best weapons to use against a werewolf, it is important to prepare yourself for the battle. This means arming yourself with the right weapons and armor. Silver weapons and armor are the best choice when it comes to battling a werewolf, as they can penetrate the werewolf's thick hide and cause them pain. It is also important to make sure that you have plenty of holy water and wolfsbane on hand, as these can be used to weaken the werewolf and make it easier to kill.

When you are ready to battle the werewolf, it is important to make sure that you are in a safe location. Werewolves are fast and powerful creatures, so it is important to make sure that you are not in an area that is too open or too crowded. Once you have found a safe location, it is important to make sure that you are well-prepared for the battle. Make sure that you have your weapons and armor ready, as well as plenty of holy water and wolfsbane.

Once you are ready to battle the werewolf, it is important to remember that werewolves are not invincible. They can be killed, and it is important to stay focused and determined throughout the battle. It is also important to remember that werewolves are sensitive to silver, so it is important to use silver weapons and armor when possible. Additionally, it is important to use holy water and wolfsbane to weaken the werewolf and make it easier to kill.

Killing a werewolf is no easy task, and it is important to take the proper precautions when attempting to do so. It is important to understand the werewolf's weaknesses, as well as to make sure that you are well-prepared for the battle. Additionally, it is important to remember that werewolves are not invincible and can be killed. With the right preparation and the right weapons, it is possible to successfully kill a werewolf.

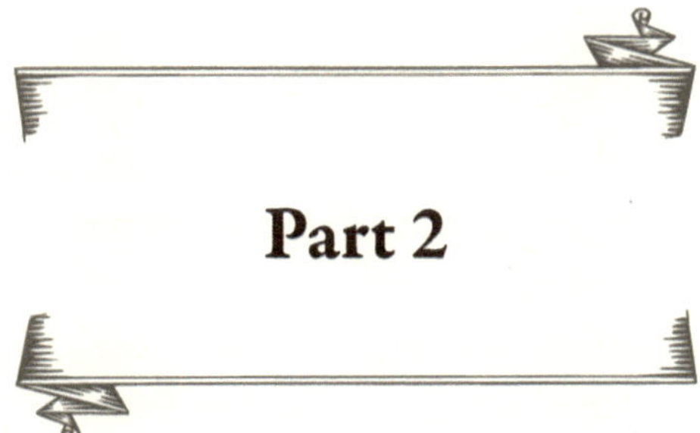

# Part 2

# Zombies

# Zombies

1.

Zombies have become a popular topic in recent years, with films, television shows, and video games portraying them as the undead walking among us. But what exactly are zombies? To answer this question, it's important to look at the various definitions of the term as well as the cultural history behind them.

In its most general definition, a zombie is a reanimated corpse that has been brought back to life with some form of supernatural power. Zombies are typically depicted as mindless, shambling creatures that are driven by an insatiable hunger for human flesh. They are usually portrayed as being slow and clumsy, but can be surprisingly fast and agile when provoked. Zombies are also usually portrayed as having an insatiable appetite for brains, although this is not always the case.

The term "zombie" has its origins in Haitian folklore, where the living dead were believed to be able to be controlled by a voodoo master. In the early 20th century, horror films began to use the zombie trope, and since then, the undead have become a staple of the horror genre.

The modern zombie is often portrayed as a result of a virus or infection that causes the dead to reanimate, often with a craving for human flesh. This is often used as a metaphor for the dangers of unchecked consumerism and the dangers of a society that is becoming increasingly disconnected from nature. Zombies are also often used as a metaphor for the dangers of unchecked technology, as they are often portrayed as being created by some form of artificial intelligence or science gone wrong.

In recent years, zombies have been used to explore themes of morality, as well as to create suspense and excitement in films, television shows, and video games. Zombies can also be used to explore the idea of death and the afterlife, as well as to explore themes of survival and the human condition.

No matter how you define them, zombies are an integral part of popular culture and have become a part of our collective consciousness. Whether they are used to explore themes of morality or to create suspense and excitement, zombies are here to stay.

2.

Killing a zombie is no easy feat. Zombies are undead creatures that have been brought back to life through a mysterious virus or other unnatural means. Zombies are incredibly resilient and difficult to kill. They have no fear of death, and can even regenerate from fatal wounds. To make matters worse, they have an insatiable hunger for human flesh. So, how do you kill a zombie?

The most effective way to kill a zombie is to destroy its brain. Zombies are reanimated corpses, and their brains are the source of their unnatural life. Destroying the brain will end the zombie's existence. This can be done in a variety of ways, such as shooting the zombie in the head, using a blunt object to crush its skull, or using a sharp object to penetrate its brain. All of these methods require a great deal of precision and accuracy, as even a minor miss can cause the zombie to remain alive and still pose a threat.

Another way to kill a zombie is to use fire. Fire is an incredibly effective weapon against zombies, as it not only destroys their bodies, but also deprives them of oxygen. It is important to note, however, that fire can be difficult to use in confined spaces or against multiple zombies. Additionally, fire can be difficult to control, and if it spreads, it can cause even more damage.

A third way to kill a zombie is to use an EMP (electromagnetic pulse) device. An EMP device emits a powerful burst of energy that disrupts and destroys electronic equipment. When used against zombies, it can disrupt their nervous systems, causing them to become disoriented and unable to move. This method is effective, but requires specialized equipment and can be difficult to use in certain situations.

Finally, it is possible to kill a zombie by simply avoiding it. Zombies are slow and clumsy, and they can easily be outrun. If you are able to stay out of their reach, they will not be able to harm you. This method is the least effective, as it requires you to remain in motion and can be difficult in certain situations, such as when you are surrounded by multiple zombies.

Killing a zombie is not an easy task. Zombies are resilient creatures that require a great deal of precision and accuracy to be taken down. The most effective way to kill a zombie is to destroy its brain, but this can be difficult to do in certain situations. Fire and EMP devices can also be used, but they can be difficult to control. Finally, it is possible to simply avoid the zombie, but this requires you to remain in motion and can be difficult in certain situations. No matter which method you choose, it is important to be aware of the risks and take the necessary precautions to ensure your safety.

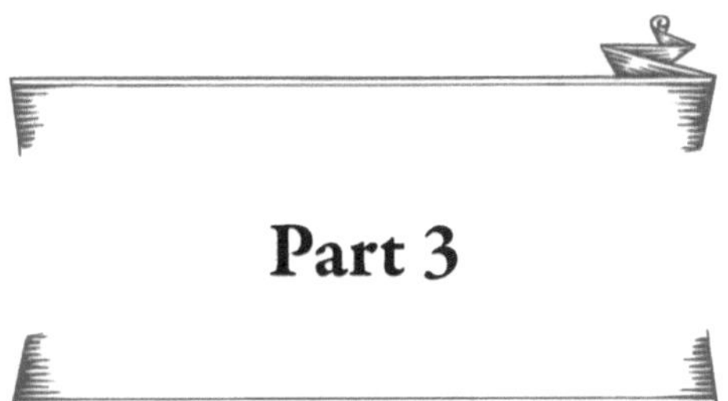

# Part 3

# vampires

# Vampires

## 1.

Vampires have been a part of our culture for centuries, with stories and legends of these mysterious creatures being told around campfires and in books. But what exactly are vampires? Are they real or just the stuff of fiction and fantasy? In this essay, we will explore what vampires are, their origins, and whether or not they exist in the real world.

At its core, the vampire is a creature that feeds on human blood, with the ability to turn its victims into vampires as well. Vampires are often depicted as pale, with long fangs and a thirst for blood. They are also often associated with the night, being able to manipulate darkness and shadows to their advantage. Vampires have also been known to have superhuman strength and speed, as well as being able to hypnotize their victims.

The origin of vampires is not entirely clear, though there are several theories as to where they came from. One theory is that vampires are a result of a curse, with some believing that a person who has committed a great sin is cursed to become a vampire. Another theory is that vampires are the result of a demonic possession, with the demon taking control of a person and turning them into a vampire.

The question of whether or not vampires exist in the real world is a difficult one to answer. On one hand, there are many stories and legends of vampires, and some people even claim to have seen them. On the other hand, there is no scientific evidence to support the existence of vampires, and no one has been able to provide any proof of their existence.

Ultimately, the answer to the question of whether or not vampires exist is up to the individual. Some may choose to believe in the existence of vampires, while others may choose to view them as nothing more than a figment of our imagination. Whatever your opinion may be, it is clear that vampires have had an impact on our culture and our imaginations for centuries.

In conclusion, vampires have been a part of our culture for centuries, with stories and legends of these mysterious creatures being told around campfires and in books. The origin of vampires is not entirely clear, though there are several theories as to where they came from. The question of whether or not vampires exist in the real world is a difficult one to answer, with some people believing in their existence and others viewing them as nothing more than a figment of our imagination. Whatever your opinion may be, it is clear that vampires have had an impact on our culture and our imaginations for centuries.

2.

Killing a vampire is no easy feat, and there are a variety of methods that have been used throughout history to do so. While some of these methods may seem outlandish, there is actually a great deal of evidence to suggest that they can be effective. In order to understand how to kill a vampire, it is important to first understand what a vampire is and what makes them so difficult to kill.

A vampire is a creature that is said to feed on the life force of the living. It is believed that vampires are able to survive by drinking the blood of humans or animals, and that they can also absorb energy from the living through physical contact. Vampires are said to be immortal, and they are often associated with the supernatural.

The difficulty in killing a vampire lies in the fact that they are, by their very nature, immortal. This means that traditional methods of killing, such as using a stake or a sword, will not be effective. Furthermore, many vampires possess enhanced strength and speed, making them difficult to catch and even more difficult to kill.

Fortunately, there are some methods that have been used throughout history to successfully kill a vampire. One of the most popular methods is to use a wooden stake to pierce the vampire's heart. This is believed to be a particularly effective method, as it will instantly stop the vampire's heart and prevent them from coming back to life.

Another method that has been used to kill a vampire is to expose them to sunlight. This is believed to be an effective method because vampires are said to be vulnerable to sunlight. If a vampire is exposed to direct sunlight, it is believed that they will burn up and be destroyed.

A third method that has been used to kill a vampire is to use holy water or a crucifix. It is believed that vampires are vulnerable to holy water and the power of the cross, and that it can be used to weaken or even kill them.

Finally, garlic has been used as a method of killing a vampire. It is believed that garlic is a powerful repellent to vampires, and that it can be used to keep them away from a person or place. It is also believed that garlic can be used to weaken a vampire, making them easier to kill.

Overall, there are a variety of methods that have been used throughout history to kill a vampire. While some of these methods may seem outlandish, there is actually a great deal of evidence to suggest that they can be effective. In order to successfully kill a vampire, it is important to understand what a vampire is and what makes them so difficult to kill. Once this is done, it is possible to use methods such as wooden stakes, sunlight, holy water, and garlic to successfully kill a vampire.

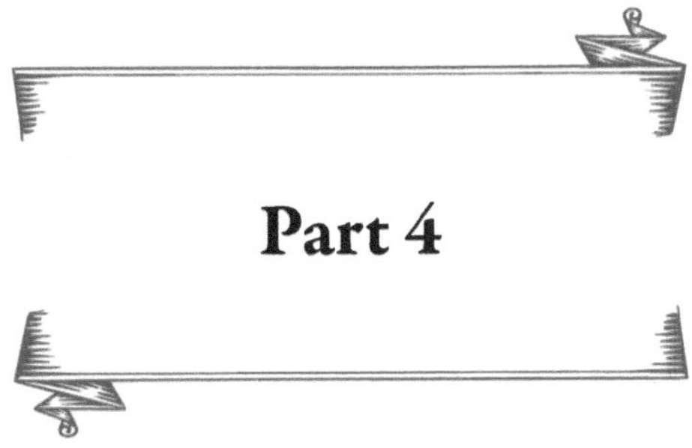

# Part 4

# Scylla

# Scylla

1.

A scylla is a mythical creature from Greek mythology that is often described as a sea monster. The scylla is typically depicted as a female creature with multiple heads and a long tail. It is said to inhabit the rocks near the Strait of Messina, between Italy and Sicily.

The scylla is first mentioned in Homer's Odyssey, where it is described as a monster that lives on one side of a narrow channel of water, opposite the whirlpool Charybdis. The scylla was said to have six heads and twelve feet, and each of its heads had three rows of sharp teeth. It was said to snatch sailors from their ships as they passed by, and devour them.

The origins of the scylla are unclear, but some believe it was inspired by the dangerous rocks near the Strait of Messina. It is possible that the scylla was a personification of these rocks, which were known to be difficult to navigate and often caused shipwrecks.

In some versions of the story, the scylla was said to have been transformed from a beautiful woman named Scylla. According to these tales, Scylla was a nymph who was loved by the sea god Glaucus. But Glaucus' former lover, the sea goddess Circe, was jealous of Scylla and turned her into a sea monster.

The scylla is often associated with the whirlpool Charybdis, which is said to be on the other side of the Strait of Messina. In the Odyssey, Odysseus is warned to avoid both the scylla and the Charybdis, as they are both too dangerous to pass.

The scylla is a popular figure in literature, appearing in works such as Dante's Inferno and John Milton's Paradise Lost. The scylla is also a popular figure in art, appearing in works such as Gustave

Doré's engraving of the Odyssey and John William Waterhouse's painting of Circe and Scylla.

In modern times, the scylla is often used as a metaphor for something that is difficult to navigate, such as a difficult decision or a dangerous situation. It is also used to describe a person or situation that is dangerous and difficult to avoid.

Overall, the scylla is a powerful figure in Greek mythology that has endured for centuries. It is a symbol of danger and difficulty, and is often used as a metaphor for something that is difficult to navigate. The scylla is also a popular figure in literature and art, appearing in works such as Dante's Inferno and John William Waterhouse's painting of Circe and Scylla.

2.

Killing a Scylla is no easy feat. This mythical sea monster has been the bane of sailors and fishermen for centuries, and it remains one of the most feared creatures of the deep even today. While some may think it is impossible to slay a Scylla, there are actually a few methods that can be used to get rid of this beast.

The first way to kill a Scylla is to use brute force. This method requires a great deal of strength and courage, as the Scylla is an incredibly powerful creature. One would need to arm themselves with a sharp weapon, such as a sword or spear, and use it to attack the Scylla. It is important to note that this method is not without risk, as the Scylla has the ability to cause great harm to its attacker.

The second way to kill a Scylla is to use magical means. This method requires a great deal of knowledge and skill, as it involves using spells and charms to defeat the creature. The person attempting to kill the Scylla must know the right spells and charms to use, and they must be able to cast them correctly. This method is not without risk either, as the Scylla is capable of using its own magic to protect itself from harm.

The third way to kill a Scylla is to use a combination of both brute force and magical means. This method requires a great deal of planning and preparation, as one must be able to use both methods in order to defeat the creature. This method is the most difficult of the three, as it requires the most skill and knowledge.

No matter which method is chosen to kill a Scylla, it is important to remember that this creature is incredibly powerful and dangerous. It is not something to be taken lightly, and it is important to be prepared for the worst. It is also important to remember that the Scylla can be killed, but it will not be easy. It will take a great deal of courage, strength, and skill in order to defeat this beast.

In conclusion, killing a Scylla is no easy task. It requires a great deal of courage, strength, and skill to defeat this powerful creature. While it may be possible to use brute force, magical means, or a combination of both, it is important to remember that the Scylla is an incredibly powerful creature and should not be taken lightly. With the right preparation and knowledge, however, it is possible to defeat this mythical beast and reclaim the seas.

# Part 5

# The Minotaur

# Minotaur
## 1.

The Minotaur is a mythical creature with a human body and the head of a bull. It is most famously featured in Greek mythology, where it is said to live in a labyrinth on the island of Crete. The Minotaur is a fearsome creature that is known for devouring humans, especially young men and women who are sent into the labyrinth as a sacrifice.

The story of the Minotaur is first mentioned in Homer's Odyssey, where it is described as a "monstrous creature" that is "half man and half bull". The Minotaur is said to have been born from a union between Pasiphae, the wife of King Minos, and a white bull sent to the king by Poseidon. After its birth, Minos had the creature imprisoned in a labyrinth designed by the architect Daedalus, where it was intended to remain forever.

The Minotaur was eventually slain by the hero Theseus, who was sent to Crete by King Aegeus of Athens to slay the creature. Theseus was able to find his way through the labyrinth with the help of a ball of thread given to him by Ariadne, the daughter of Minos. After entering the labyrinth, Theseus was able to slay the Minotaur with his sword.

The Minotaur is often used as a symbol of power, strength, and danger. It is often used to represent a challenge that must be overcome in order to achieve success. It can also be seen as a symbol of the dangers of unchecked power, as Minos was able to use the creature to control the people of Crete.

The Minotaur is also seen as a symbol of the power of the gods. The creature was born from a union between a mortal woman and a divine bull, and it is often seen as a reminder of the power of the gods over mortals. It is also a reminder of the consequences of challenging the gods, as Minos's attempt to hide the creature in the labyrinth was ultimately unsuccessful.

In modern culture, the Minotaur is often used as a symbol of power and danger. It is often featured in films, books, and video games as a powerful and dangerous creature. It is also featured in art, where it is often depicted as a powerful and dangerous creature.

The Minotaur is a powerful and fearsome creature that has been featured in mythology for centuries. Its story is a reminder of the power of the gods, the consequences of unchecked power, and the strength and courage needed to overcome challenges. The creature is also a powerful symbol of power, strength, and danger in modern culture.

2.

Killing a Minotaur is no easy task. This legendary creature of Greek mythology is half man and half bull, and is known for its strength and ferocity. It is said that the Minotaur is so powerful that it can only be slain by a hero of extraordinary skill and courage. So, how exactly do you kill a Minotaur?

There are several strategies that have been proposed over the years. One of the most famous is the story of Theseus, a hero from Greek mythology who killed the Minotaur in the Labyrinth of Crete. Theseus was given a ball of thread by the goddess Athena, which he used to find his way through the Labyrinth. Once he reached the center, he confronted the Minotaur and managed to slay it with his sword.

Another suggested strategy is to use a bow and arrow. This method requires a great deal of skill and accuracy, as the Minotaur is known to be a fast and agile creature. If the archer can hit the Minotaur in its vulnerable spots, such as its eyes, then it can be killed. However, this method can be difficult to pull off, especially if the archer is inexperienced.

Another option is to use a spear or some other type of long-range weapon. This method requires a great deal of strength and accuracy, as the Minotaur is known to be resilient and difficult to hit. If the spear is thrown with enough force and accuracy, it can be used to pierce the Minotaur's hide and kill it.

Finally, some suggest that the best way to kill a Minotaur is to use a combination of weapons. This could include a spear, a bow and arrow, and a sword. This strategy requires a great deal of skill and coordination, as the Minotaur is known to be a formidable opponent. The hero must be able to use all of these weapons in tandem in order to successfully slay the Minotaur.

No matter which strategy is used, it is clear that killing a Minotaur requires a great deal of skill and courage. It is a task that should not be taken lightly, as the Minotaur is a powerful creature of myth and legend. If a hero is brave enough to take on this challenge, then they can be sure that they will have earned the admiration and respect of their peers.

# Part 6

# Bogeyman

# Bogeyman
## 1.

The Bogeyman is a mythical creature that has been passed down through generations of folklore, often used to scare children into behaving. While the Bogeyman does not actually exist, the stories of his existence have been used to scare children for centuries. The Bogeyman is a figure of fear and mystery, and his presence has been felt in many cultures throughout the world.

The Bogeyman is usually described as a dark, mysterious figure, often wearing a hood or mask. He is said to lurk in the shadows, waiting to snatch up misbehaving children and take them away to an unknown fate. He may also be described as a tall, thin figure with long arms and legs, and a sharp, menacing smile. He is often associated with the dark of night, and is sometimes said to have glowing eyes.

The origins of the Bogeyman are unclear, but it is believed that he first appeared in the 16th century. The term "bogeyman" is thought to be derived from the Middle English word "bogge", which means "goblin". The first recorded mention of the Bogeyman was in a 15th-century English ballad called "The Bogeyman". This song tells the story of a man who is chased by a bogeyman, and the song is still sung by some people today.

The Bogeyman has been used to scare children into behaving for centuries. Parents and other adults would use the threat of the Bogeyman to encourage children to do what they were told, and to stay away from dangerous situations. The Bogeyman was also used as a way to explain away the fears and anxieties that children experience, and to help them understand the consequences of their actions.

The Bogeyman has also been used in literature and art, often as a symbol of fear and dread. In the 19th century, the Bogeyman was featured in many horror stories, often as a figure of terror and dread. In the 20th century, the Bogeyman was used in films and television shows, and he continues to be a popular figure of fear and mystery.

The Bogeyman is a figure of fear and mystery, and his presence has been felt in many cultures throughout the world. He is a symbol of the unknown, and he has been used to scare children into behaving for centuries. The Bogeyman has also been used in literature and art, often as a symbol of fear and dread. It is unclear where the Bogeyman originated, but he has been a part of folklore for centuries and is likely to remain so for many years to come.

2.

Killing the bogeyman is a daunting task. After all, the bogeyman is a mythical creature that has been used to scare children for centuries. But if you're determined to rid yourself of this creature, there are a few steps you can take to make it happen.

The first step is to understand what the bogeyman is. The bogeyman is a creature that has been used to scare children for centuries and is often associated with nightmares and dark places. It is a creature of fear and can take many forms, such as a monster, a witch, or a ghost. It is often described as having long claws, sharp teeth, and glowing eyes.

The second step is to identify the source of the bogeyman. It is important to understand why the bogeyman is haunting you. Is it because of something you did or said? Or is it because of something that happened in your past? Once you have identified the source of the bogeyman, you can begin to take steps to rid yourself of it.

The third step is to confront the bogeyman. This can be a difficult step, as it requires you to face your fears and confront the bogeyman head on. You may want to enlist the help of a friend or family member to help you in this process. Once you have confronted the bogeyman, you can begin to take steps to banish it from your life.

The fourth step is to create a plan of action. This plan should include ways to rid yourself of the bogeyman, such as avoiding dark places, keeping your home well-lit, and avoiding any activities that might attract the bogeyman. You should also make sure to take steps to protect yourself from the bogeyman, such as carrying a flashlight and wearing protective clothing.

The fifth step is to take action. Once you have created a plan of action, it is important to follow through and take action. This could include using protective charms, such as a crucifix or a garlic necklace, to ward off the bogeyman. You may also want to enlist the help of a professional, such as a priest or a witch doctor, to help you rid yourself of the bogeyman.

The sixth and final step is to stay vigilant. Even after you have taken steps to rid yourself of the bogeyman, it is important to remain vigilant and keep an eye out for any signs of its presence. You should also continue to take steps to protect yourself from the bogeyman, such as keeping your home well-lit and avoiding any activities that might attract the bogeyman.

Killing the bogeyman is no easy task, but it is possible. By understanding what the bogeyman is, identifying its source, confronting it, creating a plan of action, taking action, and staying vigilant, you can rid yourself of this creature and reclaim your peace of mind.

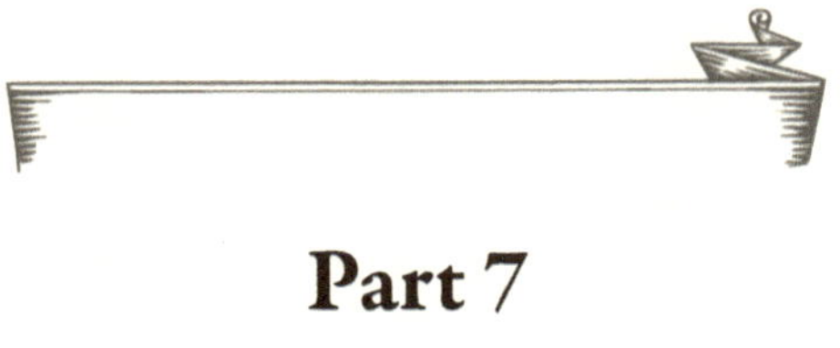

# Part 7

# Dybbuk

# Dybbuk
### 1.

A dybbuk is a spirit or ghost in Jewish mythology, often associated with possession. The word itself comes from the Hebrew root "davak," meaning to cling or attach, and is used to describe a spirit that has taken possession of a living person or object. The dybbuk is believed to be the soul of a dead person, usually someone who died suddenly or tragically, that has not yet been able to ascend to Heaven.

In Jewish folklore, dybbuks are believed to be able to possess the living, causing physical and mental illnesses and speaking through the possessed person. The dybbuk is also believed to be able to possess objects, such as books or furniture, and cause them to move or make noises. Dybbuks are believed to be able to cause harm to the living, and some stories tell of dybbuks that will not leave until their demands are met.

The belief in dybbuks dates back to ancient times, and is found in many different cultures. In some cultures, such as Jewish and Slavic, dybbuks are believed to be the souls of the dead, while in others, such as Chinese and Japanese, they are believed to be malicious spirits.

The most famous story of a dybbuk is the Yiddish play "The Dybbuk," written by S. Ansky in 1916. The play tells the story of a young woman who is possessed by the spirit of her dead lover, a dybbuk. The play is a classic of Jewish literature and has been adapted into several movies, including the classic film "The Dybbuk" (1937) by Michał Waszyński.

In modern times, the belief in dybbuks has been largely forgotten, though some still believe in their existence. For those who do, there are various ways to deal with a dybbuk, such as prayers, rituals, and exorcisms. Some believe that a dybbuk can only be removed through the intervention of a rabbi or other religious leader.

In conclusion, a dybbuk is a spirit or ghost in Jewish mythology that is believed to be able to possess the living and objects. The belief in dybbuks dates back to ancient times and is found in many different cultures. The most famous story of a dybbuk is the Yiddish play "The Dybbuk," written by S. Ansky in 1916. In modern times, the belief in dybbuks has been largely forgotten, though some still believe in their existence. For those who do, there are various ways to deal with a dybbuk, such as prayers, rituals, and exorcisms.

2.

It is said that a dybbuk is a malicious spirit that can enter the body of a living person and take control of their actions. This spirit is believed to be the soul of a dead person who has not yet been able to rest in peace. Killing a dybbuk is a difficult and complex task, as it is not a physical being, but rather a spiritual one.

To begin, it is important to understand the nature of a dybbuk. A dybbuk is believed to be a spirit that has been released from the afterlife and is seeking revenge or justice for a wrong that was done to it in life. It is believed that a dybbuk is able to enter the body of a living person and take control of their actions in order to fulfill its mission. This means that the dybbuk is not a physical being, but rather an intangible spirit that exists in the spiritual realm.

In order to kill a dybbuk, one must first understand how it works and how to combat it. The traditional way to kill a dybbuk is to use a ritual known as the Kabbalistic exorcism. This ritual is said to involve reciting special prayers and using objects that have spiritual significance, such as a cross or a Star of David. The ritual is said to be effective in banishing the dybbuk from the living person and sending it back to the afterlife.

In addition to the Kabbalistic exorcism, there are other methods that can be used to kill a dybbuk. One of these methods is to use a special amulet or talisman that is believed to have the power to ward off evil spirits. These amulets are usually made of silver and are inscribed with symbols or words that are believed to have spiritual significance. The amulet is said to be effective in repelling the dybbuk and sending it back to the afterlife.

Another method that can be used to kill a dybbuk is to use a special incantation. This incantation is believed to have the power to bind the spirit of the dybbuk and prevent it from entering the body of a living person. The incantation is said to be effective in banishing the dybbuk and sending it back to the afterlife.

Finally, another method that can be used to kill a dybbuk is to use a ritual known as the Kabbalistic banishment. This ritual is said to involve reciting special prayers and using objects that have spiritual significance, such as a cross or a Star of David. The ritual is said to be effective in banishing the dybbuk from the living person and sending it back to the afterlife.

Killing a dybbuk is a difficult and complex task, as it is not a physical being, but rather a spiritual one. In order to be successful, one must understand the nature of the dybbuk and how to combat it. Traditional methods such as the Kabbalistic exorcism, the use of amulets and talismans, and the use of incantations and rituals can all be used to effectively banish a dybbuk and send it back to the afterlife. It is important to note, however, that these methods are not always successful and that it is possible for a dybbuk to return. Therefore, it is important to be prepared and to be aware of the potential risks associated with attempting to kill a dybbuk.

# Part 8

# Banshee

# Banshee
## 1.

A banshee is a mythical creature that is believed to be an omen of death in Irish folklore. The banshee is a female spirit whose wailing is said to foretell the death of a family member. It is believed that the banshee will appear to members of certain Irish families when a death is near. The traditional description of a banshee is that of a female spirit with long, flowing white hair and a grey cloak. She is often seen as a harbinger of death, but she is also thought to be a protector of the family.

The origins of the banshee can be traced back to Celtic mythology, where she is known as a bean-sídhe or "woman of the fairy mounds." In Irish folklore, she is believed to be the spirit of a woman who died in childbirth or was murdered, and her wailing is said to be a warning of impending death. The banshee is also believed to be a messenger from the otherworld, and her wailing is said to be a sign that someone has died or is about to die.

The banshee is often described as a beautiful woman with long, flowing white hair and a grey cloak. She is said to have a sorrowful face and to be weeping tears of sorrow. In some stories, she is seen as a beautiful young woman with wings, while in others she is an old hag with a long, grey beard. She is sometimes seen as a solitary figure, while in other stories she is accompanied by a group of women called "the banshee sisters."

The banshee is believed to be a messenger from the otherworld, and her wailing is said to be a sign that someone has died or is about to die. It is said that when the banshee appears, death is imminent. In some stories, the banshee is said to appear at the bedside of a dying person, while in others she is seen in the form of a bird or a white horse.

The banshee is said to be a protectress of the family, and her wailing is said to be a warning to those who wish to harm the family. It is believed that when the banshee appears, she brings peace and comfort to the family. She is also said to be a messenger from the otherworld, and her wailing is said to be a sign that someone has died or is about to die.

The banshee is an important figure in Irish folklore, and her wailing is said to be a warning of impending death. She is believed to be a messenger from the otherworld, and her wailing is said to be a sign that someone has died or is about to die. The banshee is said to be a protectress of the family, and her wailing is said to be a warning to those who wish to harm the family. She is also believed to be a messenger from the otherworld, and her wailing is said to be a sign that someone has died or is about to die. The banshee is an important figure in Irish folklore, and her wailing is said to be a warning of impending death.

2.

Killing a Banshee is no easy task. A Banshee is a mythical creature from Irish folklore that is said to be a harbinger of death. Their wails are said to be a sign that someone is about to die. As such, they are incredibly powerful and difficult to kill. However, it is possible to do so with the right knowledge and preparation.

The first step in killing a Banshee is to acquire the right tools. For this, you will need a silver weapon of some kind, such as a sword, a dagger, or even a crossbow. Silver is said to be the only metal that can penetrate the Banshee's supernatural defenses. You will also need some kind of magical protection, such as a charm, a talisman, or a spell.

Once you have the necessary tools, you must then locate the Banshee. This can be difficult, as they are said to be able to cloak themselves in invisibility. However, they are also said to be attracted to certain places, such as graveyards, battlefields, and other places of death. If you can find one of these locations, you may be able to find the Banshee.

Once you have located the Banshee, you must then prepare yourself for battle. It is important to be calm and collected, as the Banshee's wails can cause fear and confusion. You must also be sure to keep your silver weapon at the ready, as the Banshee will use its powers to try to disarm you.

Once you are ready, you must then confront the Banshee. It is important to remember that it is a powerful creature, and you must be prepared to fight it. You must be sure to stay out of the Banshee's reach, as it can use its wail to cause fear and confusion. You must also be sure to aim your silver weapon at the Banshee's heart, as this is the only way to kill it.

Once you have struck the Banshee with your silver weapon, it is important to be sure that it is dead. This can be done by checking for a pulse or by looking for signs of life. If the Banshee is still alive, you must be sure to strike it again with your silver weapon until it is dead.

Killing a Banshee is no easy task, but it can be done with the right knowledge and preparation. You must be sure to acquire the right tools, locate the Banshee, and prepare yourself for battle. You must also be sure to aim your silver weapon at the Banshee's heart and to check for signs of life after you have struck it. By following these steps, you can successfully kill a Banshee and protect yourself from its wail.

# Part 9

# Pontianak

# Pontianak

1.

A pontianak is a type of supernatural creature found in Southeast Asian folklore. It is most commonly associated with Malaysian culture and is believed to be the spirit of a woman who died during childbirth. The pontianak is said to haunt and terrorize those who cross its path, and is often described as a pale-faced woman with long black hair, wearing a white dress.

In Malaysian folklore, the pontianak is said to be the spirit of a woman who died while pregnant or in childbirth. It is believed that the woman's spirit is unable to rest until she is avenged, and so she takes the form of a vengeful spirit. The pontianak is said to haunt the places where the woman died, and she is also said to appear to those who cross her path and seek revenge.

The pontianak is said to be able to take on many forms, including that of a beautiful woman, a bat, or a tiger. It is believed that the pontianak can cause sickness and death, and it is said that those who cross its path will become ill or die. The pontianak is also believed to be able to fly and to be able to move quickly from one place to another.

The pontianak is said to be particularly active during the night, when it is believed to be searching for its revenge. It is said that the pontianak can be seen in the form of a woman, and that she will be wearing a white dress. It is also believed that the pontianak will make a loud, high-pitched wailing sound when it is near.

There are various ways to ward off a pontianak, including offering food or prayers to the spirit. It is also believed that the pontianak can be scared away by the sound of a rooster crowing or by the sound of a bell ringing. In some cases, it is also believed that the pontianak can be driven away by the smell of incense.

In some cases, it is believed that the pontianak can be summoned and controlled by a shaman or witch doctor. It is believed that the pontianak can be used to do the bidding of the summoner, and it is said that the pontianak can be used to bring good luck or to cause harm.

The pontianak is an important part of Southeast Asian folklore, and it is believed to be the spirit of a woman who died during childbirth. It is said to haunt and terrorize those who cross its path, and it is believed that it can cause sickness and death. There are various ways to ward off a pontianak, including offering food or prayers to the spirit, and it is believed that the pontianak can be summoned and controlled by a shaman or witch doctor. The pontianak is an important part of Southeast Asian folklore, and it is believed to be a powerful and dangerous creature.

2.

Killing a pontianak, a type of vampiric ghost in Malaysian and Indonesian folklore, is no easy task. It is said that these creatures are powerful and resilient, and it can take a great deal of effort to put an end to their existence. As with many supernatural creatures, there is no one-size-fits-all approach to killing a pontianak, but there are certain steps that can be taken to increase the chances of success.

The first step to killing a pontianak is to understand what they are and where they come from. A pontianak is a female ghost originating from Malaysian and Indonesian folklore. They are said to be the spirits of women who died during childbirth or were killed by violence. It is believed that these spirits are vengeful and will seek out revenge against those who wronged them in life.

In order to kill a pontianak, it is important to understand the specific characteristics of the particular pontianak in question. This includes knowing the type of weapon that can be used against them, the conditions that must be met in order for the weapon to be effective, and any special rituals that may be necessary to complete the task.

One of the most common weapons used to kill a pontianak is a kris, a type of dagger with a wavy blade. It is said that the kris must be made from iron or steel and must be blessed by a priest or shaman before it can be used effectively. In addition, the kris must be held in the right hand and pointed at the pontianak in order to be effective.

In addition to the kris, there are other weapons that can be used to kill a pontianak. These include a sharpened bamboo stake, a silver bullet, or a blessed knife. It is important to note, however, that these weapons may not be effective against all pontianaks. It is important to research the particular pontianak in question in order to determine which weapon will be most effective.

In addition to the weapons used to kill a pontianak, there are also certain rituals that must be performed in order to ensure success. For instance, it is said that a pontianak can only be killed if the person attempting to do so is wearing a white robe and is carrying a white cloth. The white robe symbolizes purity and the white cloth is said to represent the pontianak's soul.

Finally, it is important to remember that killing a pontianak is not an easy task. It requires a great deal of effort and courage, and the outcome is never guaranteed. It is important to be prepared and to understand the risks involved before attempting to kill a pontianak. With the right knowledge and preparation, however, it is possible to successfully put an end to the existence of these vampiric ghosts.

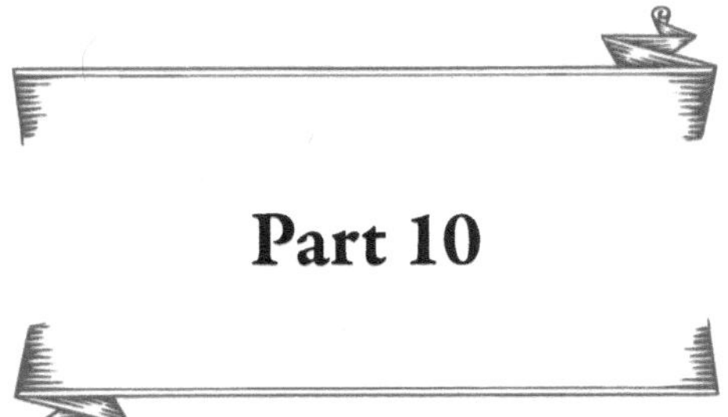

# Part 10

# Hydra

# Hydra

### 1.

A hydra is a fascinating creature that can be found in freshwater ponds and streams. It is a small, freshwater invertebrate that belongs to the phylum Cnidaria, which also includes jellyfish and corals. The most recognizable feature of the hydra is its tubular body that can reach a length of up to 2 cm. It has a mouth at the end of its body and tentacles that surround the mouth.

The hydra is an interesting creature that has some unique characteristics. For one, it is a polyp, which means it is a sessile organism that attaches itself to a substrate. It does not move around like other animals, but instead, it uses its tentacles to catch food and to move itself.

The hydra is also able to regenerate itself. If it is cut in half, it can regenerate the missing part. This process of regeneration is known as budding and it allows the hydra to reproduce asexually.

The hydra is an incredibly important organism in the aquatic food chain. It is a primary consumer and an important source of food for many other animals. It feeds on small organisms such as plankton and other tiny invertebrates. It also serves as a food source for larger animals such as fish.

The hydra is an amazing creature that has been studied for centuries. It is an important part of the aquatic ecosystem and it is a fascinating creature to observe in its natural environment. Its ability to regenerate itself and its important role in the food chain make it an interesting organism to study.

### 2.

Killing a hydra, a mythical creature from Greek mythology, is no easy feat. For centuries, people have been trying to find ways to defeat this seemingly immortal creature. Fortunately, there are a few methods that can be employed to slay the beast. In this essay, we will explore how to kill a hydra, including the strategies that have been used successfully in the past.

The most famous example of a successful hydra-slaying attempt comes from the story of Heracles. In this myth, Heracles was tasked with slaying the beast as one of his twelve labors. He was able to do this by using a combination of strategy and brute force. First, he used a burning torch to cauterize the neck of the hydra after he had cut off one of its heads. This prevented the hydra from regenerating new heads. Then, Heracles used his club to smash the remaining heads.

The use of fire to prevent regeneration is a key element in the successful slaying of a hydra. This method has been used by many other heroes in Greek mythology, including Perseus and Bellerophon. The fire cauterizes the wound, preventing the hydra from regenerating new heads. This strategy can be used in conjunction with other methods, such as smashing the remaining heads with a club or weapon.

In addition to the use of fire, there are other methods that can be used to slay the hydra. One such method is to use poison. This can be done by coating a weapon with a deadly poison, such as the venom of a snake or scorpion. When the weapon is used to strike the hydra, the poison will spread throughout its body, eventually killing it.

Another method is to use a magical weapon. These weapons are imbued with special powers, such as the ability to kill the hydra instantly. This method was used by the hero Theseus in Greek mythology. He used a magical sword to slay the hydra, thus proving his strength and courage.

Finally, there is the use of a magical herb. This herb is said to have the power to kill the hydra instantly. This method was used by the hero Cadmus in Greek mythology. He crushed the herb and spread it over the body of the hydra, causing it to die instantly.

Overall, slaying a hydra is no easy feat. It requires a combination of strategy and brute force. The most successful methods involve the use of fire, poison, magical weapons, and magical herbs. By employing one or more of these methods, a hero can successfully slay the hydra and prove his strength and courage.

# Part 11

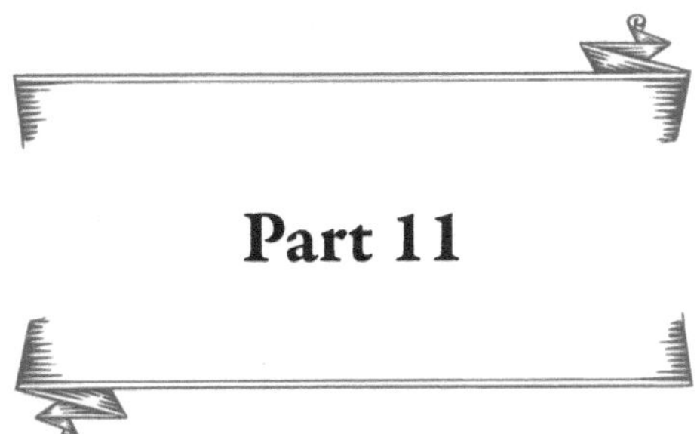

# Yeti, Sasquatch or Bigfoot

# Yeti, Sasquatch or Bigfoot

### 1.

The Yeti, also known as the Abominable Snowman, is a mythical creature that has been a part of folklore and myth for centuries. It is said to inhabit the Himalayan mountains in Nepal and Tibet, and is described as a large, ape-like creature with white fur. The Yeti is a popular figure in popular culture, appearing in films, television shows, books, and video games.

The Yeti is believed to have originated in the folklore of the Himalayan region of Nepal and Tibet. The earliest known accounts of the Yeti date back to the early 19th century, when British mountaineers began exploring the region. The name "Yeti" is derived from the Tibetan word "yeh-teh," which means "magical creature."

The Yeti is described as a large, ape-like creature with white fur. It is typically depicted as being between six and eight feet tall, although some accounts describe it as being much larger. It is said to have a human-like face with long hair and a beard. The Yeti is said to be very strong and able to move quickly over snow and ice.

The Yeti is believed to be a solitary creature that lives in remote, mountainous regions. It is said to be shy and reclusive, and is rarely seen by humans. However, there have been numerous reports of sightings of the Yeti by both locals and Westerners.

The Yeti has become a popular figure in popular culture, appearing in films, television shows, books, and video games. It is often depicted as a friendly, yet mysterious creature, and is often used as a symbol of the unknown. In some stories, the Yeti is portrayed as a protector of the mountains, while in others it is seen as a dangerous creature that must be avoided.

The Yeti is a fascinating creature, and its mystery has captivated people for centuries. While there is no scientific evidence to support the existence of the Yeti, its legend continues to live on in the minds of those who believe in its existence. Whether it is a real creature or just a figment of our imagination, the Yeti remains an intriguing and mysterious creature that continues to fascinate people around the world.

2.

Given the yeti's mysterious nature, it is not surprising that there is no definitive answer to the question of how to kill a yeti. However, there are several theories as to how one might go about attempting to do so. One of the most popular theories is that the yeti can be killed by using a special type of weapon, such as a silver bullet or a magical weapon. This theory is based on the belief that the yeti is vulnerable to silver and magic, and that using either of these weapons will be effective in killing the creature.

Another theory is that the yeti can be killed by using fire. This theory is based on the belief that the yeti is vulnerable to fire, and that using a large fire to burn the creature will be effective in killing it. However, this theory has not been proven, and there is no scientific evidence to support it.

A third theory is that the yeti can be killed by using a powerful weapon, such as a rifle or a bow and arrow. This theory is based on the belief that the yeti is vulnerable to powerful weapons, and that using a powerful weapon will be effective in killing the creature. However, this theory has not been proven, and there is no scientific evidence to support it.

Finally, there is the theory that the yeti can be killed by using an ancient ritual. This theory is based on the belief that the yeti is vulnerable to certain rituals, and that using an ancient ritual will be effective in killing the creature. However, this theory has not been proven, and there is no scientific evidence to support it.

In conclusion, it is clear that there is no definitive answer to the question of how to kill a yeti. While there are numerous theories as to how one might go about attempting to do so, none of them have been proven, and there is no scientific evidence to support any of them. Therefore, it is best to approach the yeti with caution, as it is not known how to effectively kill the creature.

# Part 12

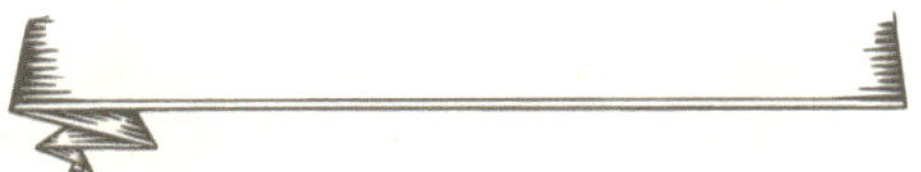

# Dragon

# Dragon
## 1.

A dragon is a mythical creature that has been part of the folklore of many cultures for centuries. Dragons are typically depicted as large, powerful, and often fearsome creatures with wings, scales, and fire-breathing capabilities. They are often associated with strength, power, and wisdom, and are often seen as symbols of good and evil, depending on the context.

The origin of the dragon is a matter of debate. Some believe that dragons originated in ancient Greece and Rome, while others attribute their origin to China or India. In any case, dragons have been part of human culture for a very long time.

In the Western world, dragons are often seen as symbols of strength and power. They are often associated with heroic deeds and protection of the innocent. In some cases, dragons are seen as symbols of evil, such as in the case of the dragon Smaug from J.R.R. Tolkien's The Hobbit.

In Chinese culture, dragons are seen as symbols of strength, power, and good luck. They are often associated with water and are seen as protectors of the people. In the Chinese zodiac, dragons are seen as a sign of luck and prosperity, and are often associated with wisdom and power.

In Japan, dragons are seen as symbols of good luck and protection. They are often associated with the sea and are seen as protectors of the people. In Japan, dragons are also seen as symbols of wisdom and power.

No matter what culture or region dragons are associated with, they are generally seen as powerful and wise creatures. They are often seen as symbols of strength, power, and protection. They are also seen as symbols of luck and prosperity.

Dragons are typically depicted as large, powerful creatures with wings, scales, and fire-breathing capabilities. They are often associated with strength, power, and wisdom, and are often seen as symbols of good and evil, depending on the context. Dragons are seen as protectors of the people, and are often associated with water and the sea. They are also seen as symbols of luck and prosperity, and are associated with wisdom and power.

Dragons have been part of human culture for centuries, and are still seen as powerful and wise creatures today. They are often seen as symbols of strength, power, and protection, and are associated with luck and prosperity. Dragons are seen as protectors of the people, and are often associated with water and the sea. Dragons are also seen as symbols of wisdom and power, and are often seen as symbols of good and evil, depending on the context.

2.

Killing a dragon, a mythical creature that has been around for centuries, is no easy task. It requires a great deal of skill, courage, and knowledge to take on such a powerful beast. Fortunately, there are several methods that have been used throughout history to slay these creatures. Depending on the type of dragon, these methods may vary, but all of them require a certain level of bravery and cunning.

The first way to kill a dragon is to use a weapon. Depending on the size and strength of the dragon, a sword or other sharp object may be necessary. A sword can be used to stab the dragon in the heart or other vulnerable areas. Even a bow and arrow may be able to penetrate the dragon's tough hide. However, it is important to remember that a dragon's scales are incredibly tough, so it may take multiple strikes to penetrate them.

A second way to kill a dragon is to use magic. Magic can be used to weaken the dragon or even to outright kill it. For example, a powerful spell can be used to freeze the dragon in place, allowing an attacker to approach and deliver a fatal blow. Other spells may be able to weaken the dragon's defenses, making it easier to slay.

A third way to kill a dragon is to use fire. Fire has long been used to combat dragons, as the flames can quickly burn through the dragon's scales. Additionally, fire can be used to create a wall of flames, which can prevent the dragon from escaping or attacking. Of course, this method is incredibly dangerous, as the fire can quickly spread and cause more damage than intended.

Finally, a fourth way to kill a dragon is to use a combination of the previous three methods. For example, a powerful spell can be used to weaken the dragon, allowing an attacker to deliver a fatal blow with a sword. Alternatively, fire can be used to weaken the dragon's defenses, allowing an attacker to use a weapon to deliver the final blow.

No matter which method is used to kill a dragon, it is important to remember that these creatures are incredibly powerful and can be very dangerous. Therefore, it is important to approach these creatures with caution and to be prepared for any outcome. Additionally, it is important to remember that dragons have been around for centuries, so it is important to respect their power and strength.

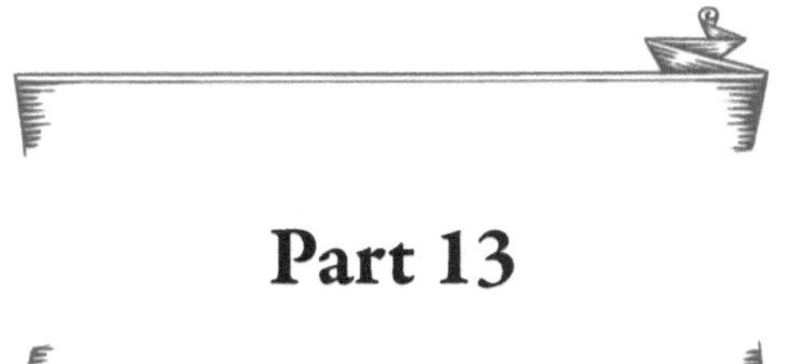

# Part 13

# Basilisk

# Basilisk
## 1.

A basilisk is a mythical creature that has been part of many cultures for centuries. It is often depicted as a reptilian creature with a crown or a serpent-like body, and is sometimes referred to as the "King of Serpents". The basilisk has been featured in many works of fiction, from Harry Potter to The Chronicles of Narnia, and is often seen as a symbol of power and strength.

The origin of the basilisk is unclear, but it is believed to have originated in Europe in the Middle Ages. It is thought to have been inspired by the Greek legend of the Chimera, a creature with the head of a lion, the body of a goat, and the tail of a serpent. The basilisk is often associated with fire and is said to have the ability to kill with its gaze.

The basilisk is believed to have a variety of powers, including the ability to turn other creatures to stone, to cause fear in its victims, and to bring death with its gaze. It is also said to be able to fly and to be immune to most weapons. The basilisk is often portrayed as a powerful and dangerous creature, but it is also seen as a symbol of strength and courage.

The basilisk has been featured in a variety of works of fiction, from Harry Potter to The Chronicles of Narnia. In Harry Potter, the basilisk is a giant serpent that can be found in the Chamber of Secrets. It is described as being able to kill with its gaze and is a powerful and dangerous creature. In The Chronicles of Narnia, the White Witch uses a basilisk to turn her enemies into stone.

In some cultures, the basilisk is seen as a symbol of power and strength. It is often seen as a protector, and is believed to have the ability to ward off evil. The basilisk is also said to have healing powers and is seen as a symbol of health and vitality.

The basilisk is a mythical creature that has been part of many cultures for centuries. It is often depicted as a reptilian creature with a crown or a serpent-like body, and is sometimes referred to as the "King of Serpents". The basilisk is believed to have a variety of powers, including the ability to turn other creatures to stone, to cause fear in its victims, and to bring death with its gaze. It is also seen as a symbol of power and strength, and is often used as a protector and symbol of health and vitality. The basilisk has been featured in a variety of works of fiction, from Harry Potter to The Chronicles of Narnia, and continues to captivate and fascinate people today.

2.

Killing a basilisk is no small feat. This creature has been feared in many cultures throughout history for its power and ferocity, and it has been the subject of many tales and legends. In the Harry Potter series, the basilisk is a giant serpent that can kill with one glance. So how do you kill a basilisk?

The most common method of killing a basilisk is to use a mirror. This method is used in the Harry Potter series, where Harry Potter uses a mirror to reflect the basilisk's gaze and make it turn on itself. This is effective because the basilisk's gaze is fatal, so by reflecting it back at itself, it is killed instantly.

Another method of killing a basilisk is to use a phoenix's tears. In the Harry Potter series, Fawkes the phoenix is able to use its tears to heal any wound, including those caused by the basilisk. The tears of a phoenix can also be used to weaken the basilisk, making it easier to kill.

A third method of killing a basilisk is to use a sword or spear. This method is used in the Harry Potter series, where Harry Potter uses a sword to stab the basilisk in the heart. This is effective because it is a direct attack on the basilisk's weak spot, and it is the only way to kill it.

Finally, a fourth method of killing a basilisk is to use a basilisk horn. This method is used in the Harry Potter series, where Harry Potter uses a basilisk horn to weaken the basilisk and make it easier to kill. The horn is effective because it emits a sound that can paralyze the basilisk, making it easier to kill.

In conclusion, killing a basilisk is no easy task. It requires special weapons and knowledge of its weaknesses. The most common methods of killing a basilisk are to use a mirror, phoenix tears, a sword or spear, or a basilisk horn. All of these methods have proven effective in the Harry Potter series, and they can be used to effectively kill a basilisk.

# Part 14

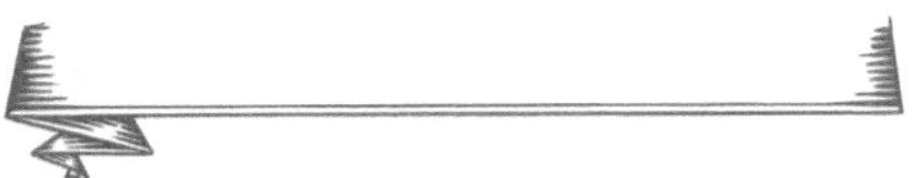

# Griffin

# Griffin
### 1.

A griffin is a mythical creature with the head, wings, and talons of an eagle, and the body of a lion. It is said to have originated in the Middle East and is often seen in the art and literature of Ancient Greece and Rome. The griffin is seen as a powerful symbol of strength, courage, and protection.

In mythology, griffins are said to be guardians of hidden treasures and sacred places. They were believed to be a symbol of divine power and were often associated with the gods. Griffins were also thought to keep away evil spirits and protect against danger. In some cultures, griffins are seen as protectors of the sun and the moon, as well as other celestial bodies.

Griffins are often depicted in art and literature as fierce and powerful creatures. They are often shown with a lion's body and an eagle's head and wings. The wings of a griffin are usually spread wide, giving them a majestic appearance. They are usually shown with a long tail, and their claws are often sharp and powerful.

In some cultures, griffins are seen as symbols of justice and truth. They are believed to be able to distinguish right from wrong and to be able to judge fairly. They are also seen as symbols of strength and courage, and are often associated with warriors and heroes.

Griffins are also seen in some cultures as symbols of wealth and prosperity. In some cultures, griffins are seen as protectors of the home, and are believed to bring good luck and prosperity to those who have them.

Griffins are also popular in modern culture. They are often used as symbols in movies, literature, and video games. They are also popular as mascots for sports teams and as logos for businesses.

The griffin is an interesting mythical creature that has been around for centuries. It is often seen as a symbol of strength, courage, protection, and justice. It is also seen as a symbol of wealth and prosperity. Griffins are popular in modern culture, and are often used as symbols in movies, literature, and video games. They are also popular as mascots for sports teams and as logos for businesses.

2.

Killing a griffin is no easy task. This mythical creature is a powerful symbol of strength and courage, and is said to have the body of a lion and the head and wings of an eagle. It has been described as a powerful and majestic creature that is not to be taken lightly. To kill a griffin, one must be prepared to face a formidable opponent and have a strategy to ensure success.

The first step in killing a griffin is to research the creature. It is important to know what type of griffin you are facing and what its weaknesses may be. Depending on the type of griffin, the weaknesses may vary. For example, some griffins are more vulnerable to fire or ice, while others may be susceptible to certain weapons. Knowing the weaknesses of the griffin is key to formulating a plan of attack.

Once you have identified the weaknesses of the griffin, the next step is to create a strategy. This should include a plan of attack, a list of supplies needed, and a method of escape. It is important to have a plan of attack that takes into account the griffin's weaknesses and the environment in which the battle will take place. For example, if the griffin is vulnerable to fire, then the plan should include the use of fire-based weapons or spells. Additionally, it is important to have a list of supplies such as weapons, armor, and potions, as well as a method of escape in case the battle does not go as planned.

When it comes to the actual battle, it is important to be prepared and have a well-thought-out strategy. It is best to attack the griffin from a distance if possible, using weapons such as bows and arrows or spells. If the griffin is vulnerable to fire, then it is a good idea to use fire-based spells or weapons. Additionally, it is important to be aware of the griffin's surroundings and use the environment to your advantage. For example, if the griffin is standing on a cliff, then it may be possible to push the creature off the edge.

Once the griffin is defeated, it is important to be prepared for the aftermath. It is best to have a plan in place for disposing of the body, as well as any loot that may be collected from the creature. Additionally, it is important to be aware of any potential consequences that may arise from killing a griffin, such as angering the gods or other mythical creatures.

Killing a griffin is no easy task. It requires research, strategy, preparation, and courage. It is important to be aware of the weaknesses of the griffin and to have a well-thought-out plan of attack. Additionally, it is important to be prepared for the aftermath and to dispose of the body properly. With the right strategy and a bit of luck, it is possible to successfully kill a griffin.

# Part 15

# Satyrs

# Satyrs
## 1.

A satyr is a creature from Greek mythology that is part human and part animal. The creature is typically depicted as having the upper body of a human and the legs and horns of a goat. Satyrs are often seen as mischievous and hedonistic creatures, and they are often associated with Dionysus, the god of wine and revelry.

Satyrs are thought to have originated in the Bronze Age, and they were believed to be the companions of Dionysus. They were often seen as the attendants of Dionysus, and they were associated with partying and revelry. They were often depicted in Greek art as playing instruments such as the flute and the syrinx.

Satyrs are often seen as symbols of nature and fertility. They are associated with the wild, untamed nature of the countryside and the forests. They are also often seen as symbols of unrestrained pleasure and hedonism. They are often seen as symbols of freedom and joy, and they represent the carefree and wild spirit of nature.

Satyrs are often seen as symbols of the human spirit. They are associated with the human desire for freedom and pleasure. They represent the wild and untamed spirit of man, and they are often seen as symbols of passion and creativity. They are often associated with the creative spirit of man, and they are seen as symbols of the human ability to create and explore.

Satyrs are often seen as symbols of fertility. They are associated with the fertility of the land, and they represent the abundance of nature. They are often seen as symbols of the natural cycle of life, and they represent the fertility of the land and the abundance of nature.

Satyrs are often seen as symbols of chaos and mischief. They are often seen as symbols of disorder and disruption, and they are seen as symbols of rebellion and anarchy. They are often seen as symbols of chaos and disorder, and they represent the wild and untamed spirit of man.

Satyrs are often seen as symbols of strength and power. They are associated with the strength and power of nature, and they are seen as symbols of the power of man. They are often seen as symbols of courage and bravery, and they represent the strength and power of man.

Satyrs are often seen as symbols of joy and celebration. They are associated with the joy and celebration of life, and they are seen as symbols of the joy and celebration of life. They are often seen as symbols of celebration and joy, and they represent the joy and celebration of life.

Satyrs are often seen as symbols of life and death. They are associated with the cycle of life and death, and they are seen as symbols of the cycle of life and death. They are often seen as symbols of the cycle of life and death, and they represent the cycle of life and death.

Satyrs are often seen as symbols of wisdom and knowledge. They are associated with the wisdom and knowledge of the gods, and they are seen as symbols of the wisdom and knowledge of the gods. They are often seen as symbols of wisdom and knowledge, and they represent the wisdom and knowledge of the gods.

Satyrs are an important part of Greek mythology and culture. They are seen as symbols of nature and fertility, of joy and celebration, of strength and power, of chaos and mischief, and of wisdom and knowledge. They are seen as symbols of the human spirit, and they represent the wild and untamed spirit of man. They are an important part of Greek mythology and culture, and they are seen as symbols of the human spirit and the cycle of life and death.

2.

These mythical creatures have been known to be immortal, making them difficult to take down. However, with the right knowledge and preparation, it is possible to successfully take down a satyr. In this essay, we will discuss the steps necessary to kill a satyr.

The first step to killing a satyr is to understand its weaknesses. Although satyrs are immortal, they do have a few weaknesses that can be exploited. It is said that satyrs are vulnerable to silver, so using a silver weapon is the most effective way to take one down. In addition, satyrs are also said to be vulnerable to holy water and blessed weapons, so these can be used to weaken the satyr before attempting to take it down.

The second step to killing a satyr is to prepare for battle. Satyrs are powerful creatures and can be difficult to take down, so it is important to be prepared for a fight. Make sure to bring plenty of silver weapons and holy water to use against the satyr, and also bring along any blessed weapons that you may have. It is also a good idea to bring along some allies to help you in the fight, as satyrs are known to be powerful opponents.

The third step to killing a satyr is to find the right location. Satyrs are known to be powerful creatures, so it is important to choose the right location for the battle. Look for a place that is open and has plenty of space for you and your allies to maneuver. Avoid enclosed spaces, as this will give the satyr an advantage.

The fourth step to killing a satyr is to use your weapons effectively. Satyrs are powerful creatures, so it is important to use your weapons to their fullest potential. Make sure to aim for the satyr's weak points, such as its head or heart. Also, make sure to use your silver and holy water weapons to weaken the satyr before attempting to take it down.

The fifth step to killing a satyr is to stay focused. Satyrs are powerful creatures and can be difficult to take down, so it is important to stay focused on the task at hand. Don't get distracted by the satyr's tricks or taunts, and keep your eyes on the prize.

Killing a satyr is no easy feat, but with the right knowledge and preparation, it is possible to successfully take one down. By understanding the satyr's weaknesses, preparing for battle, finding the right location, using weapons effectively, and staying focused, you can successfully take down a satyr. Good luck!

# Part 16

# Aqrabuamelu

## Aqrabuamelu

1. An aqrabuamelu is a type of supernatural creature with origins in ancient Mesopotamian mythology. The aqrabuamelu is described as having the head of a human and the body of a scorpion. This creature is said to be a guardian of the underworld and is believed to protect the gates of the underworld from intruders.

The aqrabuamelu is often depicted in ancient Mesopotamian art and literature, and is thought to have been a popular figure in Mesopotamian culture. The aqrabuamelu is also mentioned in the Epic of Gilgamesh, an ancient Mesopotamian poem that tells the story of the hero Gilgamesh and his quest for immortality. In the poem, the aqrabuamelu is described as a fearsome creature with the power to kill anyone who attempts to enter the underworld.

The aqrabuamelu is also referenced in other ancient texts, such as the Babylonian creation myth Enuma Elish, where the aqrabuamelu is said to have been created by the god Marduk. In this myth, Marduk is said to have created the aqrabuamelu to guard the gates of the underworld and prevent the dead from escaping.

The aqrabuamelu is also mentioned in the Book of Revelation, where it is described as a fearsome creature with a lion's head, eagle's wings, and a serpent's tail. This creature is said to be a symbol of God's power and authority over the underworld.

The aqrabuamelu has also been referenced in modern popular culture, such as in the film series The Mummy, where the aqrabuamelu is depicted as a powerful creature that guards the entrance to the underworld. In the film, the aqrabuamelu is said to be an immortal creature that can grant eternal life to those who defeat it in battle.

The aqrabuamelu is a fascinating creature with a long and varied history. Its depictions in ancient art and literature reveal a creature that was feared and respected by the people of Mesopotamia and is still remembered today in popular culture. Its symbolism of power and authority over the underworld has been used to create a powerful and memorable figure in modern storytelling. The aqrabuamelu is a fascinating creature that continues to captivate and inspire people today.

2.

Killing an Aqrabuamelu, also known as the Scorpion Man, is no easy feat. This mythical creature is said to have the body of a man and the head of a scorpion, and is said to be nearly impossible to slay. Despite the difficulty of killing an Aqrabuamelu, there are several methods that have been suggested throughout the ages.

The first and most common method of killing an Aqrabuamelu is through the use of a weapon. This could be anything from a sword to an arrow, but the weapon must be made of either copper or iron. The reason for this is that the Aqrabuamelu is said to be particularly vulnerable to weapons made of these metals. It is also important to note that the weapon must be wielded by a brave and noble warrior, as the Aqrabuamelu is said to be able to recognize courage and will spare those it deems worthy.

Another method of killing an Aqrabuamelu is through the use of magic. This is a difficult and dangerous task, as the Aqrabuamelu is said to be immune to most forms of magic. However, there are some spells and incantations that are said to be able to weaken the creature, making it easier to slay. This method is not recommended, however, as it is often difficult to find the correct spell or incantation, and it can be dangerous if done incorrectly.

A third method of killing an Aqrabuamelu is through the use of a special herb. This herb is said to be able to weaken the Aqrabuamelu, making it easier to kill. Unfortunately, this herb is incredibly rare and difficult to find. It is also said to be incredibly dangerous, as it can poison those who come in contact with it.

Finally, the fourth and most difficult method of killing an Aqrabuamelu is through the use of a sacred weapon. This weapon is said to be blessed by the gods themselves and is said to be the only weapon capable of slaying the Aqrabuamelu. Unfortunately, these weapons are incredibly rare and almost impossible to find.

No matter which method is used, killing an Aqrabuamelu is no easy task. It requires skill, bravery, and a great deal of luck. It is also important to note that, even if a warrior is successful in slaying the Aqrabuamelu, they will still be haunted by the creature's death curse. The curse is said to bring misfortune and death to anyone who kills an Aqrabuamelu, so it is important to consider this before attempting to slay the creature.

In conclusion, killing an Aqrabuamelu is no easy feat. It requires skill, bravery, and luck, and it is important to consider the consequences of slaying the creature before attempting to do so. While there are several methods that have been suggested throughout the ages, it is important to remember that none of them are guaranteed to work.

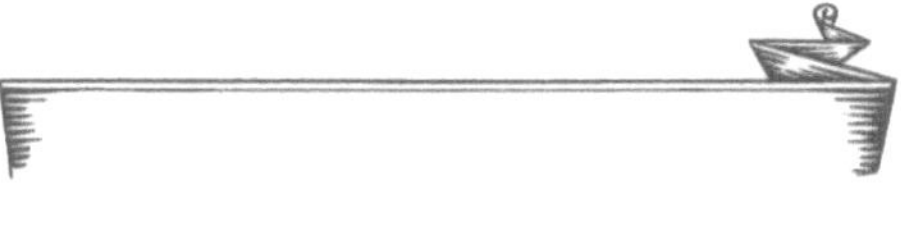

# Part 17

# Gorgon

# Gorgon
### 1.

A gorgon is a mythical creature found in ancient Greek mythology. It is typically portrayed as a female with snakes for hair and a gaze that turns onlookers to stone. The most famous gorgon is Medusa, who was slain by the hero Perseus.

The origin of the gorgon is uncertain, but it is thought to have been derived from the Greek word gorgos, which means "dreadful" or "terrible." In ancient Greek art, the gorgon was often depicted as a female with snakes for hair, sharp claws, and a terrible gaze. The gorgon was often used to symbolize danger and fear.

The gorgon was often associated with the underworld and the forces of chaos. In some stories, the gorgon was portrayed as a guardian of the underworld, protecting its secrets and warding off intruders. In other stories, the gorgon was seen as a creature of chaos and destruction, wreaking havoc wherever it went.

The most famous gorgon is Medusa, who was slain by the hero Perseus. According to the story, Medusa was once a beautiful woman who was cursed by the goddess Athena to have snakes for hair and a gaze that could turn onlookers to stone. Perseus was able to slay Medusa by using her reflection in his shield to avoid her gaze.

The gorgon was a popular figure in Greek art and literature. In the Odyssey, the gorgon is mentioned several times, and it appears in numerous works of art. The gorgon was also a popular figure in Roman art, often appearing on coins and other objects.

The gorgon has become a popular figure in modern culture as well. It is often used as a symbol of fear and danger, and it has been featured in films, video games, and other media. The gorgon is also a popular figure in fantasy and horror literature, often appearing as a powerful and dangerous creature.

The gorgon is a fascinating figure in Greek mythology. Its origins are uncertain, but it has been a popular figure in art and literature for centuries. It is often seen as a symbol of fear and danger, and it has been featured in numerous works of art and literature. The most famous gorgon is Medusa, who was slain by the hero Perseus. The gorgon is a popular figure in modern culture as well, often appearing as a symbol of fear and danger.

2.

Killing a gorgon is no easy feat, and it is certainly not for the faint of heart. A gorgon is an ancient creature from Greek mythology, often depicted as having a snake-like body, wings, and a head with either one or multiple snake heads. They are said to have the power to turn anyone who looks directly at them into stone. As such, it is no surprise that killing a gorgon is considered to be a difficult task.

One of the most famous stories of a gorgon being killed is that of Medusa, a gorgon who was slain by the hero Perseus. The story of Perseus killing Medusa is a classic example of how to kill a gorgon. According to the story, Perseus was given a set of special weapons from the gods in order to defeat Medusa, including a shield, a sword, and a helmet of invisibility. With these tools, Perseus was able to approach Medusa without her being able to see him, and then he used his sword to decapitate her.

This story is an interesting example of how to kill a gorgon, but it is not the only way. In fact, there are many different methods that can be used to kill a gorgon. One of the most common methods is to use a weapon that is specifically designed to be used against a gorgon. These weapons are often made of special metals or materials that are resistant to the petrifying gaze of a gorgon, allowing the wielder to approach and attack the creature without fear of being turned to stone.

Another option is to use a magical weapon. In some stories, magical weapons such as a bow and arrow or a spear are used to kill a gorgon. These weapons are often imbued with special powers that allow them to pierce the skin of a gorgon, allowing the user to strike the creature from a distance. This can be a useful tactic, as it allows the user to avoid the gorgon's gaze and attack it without fear of being turned to stone.

Finally, it is also possible to use a magical spell to kill a gorgon. In some stories, heroes are able to use a powerful spell to turn the gorgon to stone, thus killing it without having to approach it. This can be a difficult task, as it requires knowledge of powerful magic, but it can be an effective way to defeat a gorgon.

In conclusion, killing a gorgon is no easy feat, and it requires a great deal of courage and skill. There are several methods that can be used to kill a gorgon, including using a weapon specifically designed to be used against a gorgon, using a magical weapon, or using a powerful spell. All of these methods can be effective, depending on the situation, and can allow a hero to defeat a gorgon and save the day.

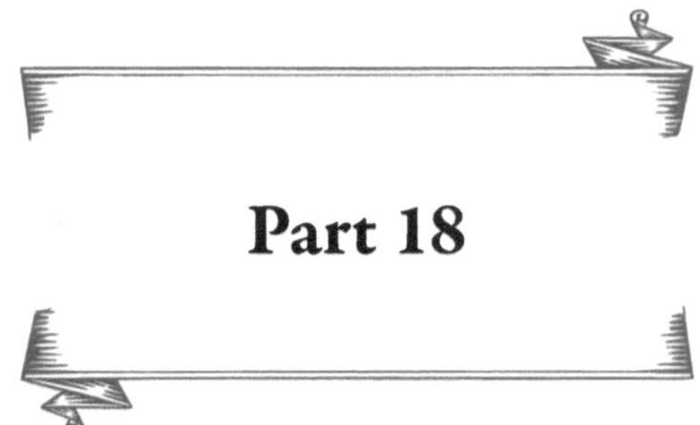

# Part 18

# Nymphs, Sprites or Faeries

# Nymphs, Sprites or Faeries
## 1.

Nymphs have long been a part of mythology and folklore, with stories of their beauty and supernatural power captivating audiences for centuries. But what exactly are nymphs? To answer this question, it is important to look at the various forms of nymphs in mythology, the characteristics they are known for, and their place in the pantheon of mythical creatures.

Nymphs are often thought of as female nature spirits, and they are closely associated with particular natural elements. In Greek mythology, for example, there are the Naiads, who are associated with bodies of fresh water such as streams, springs, and brooks; the Dryads, who are associated with trees; and the Oreads, who are associated with mountains. Other types of nymphs include the Nereids, who are associated with the sea, and the Aurae, who are associated with the wind.

In addition to being associated with natural elements, nymphs are often characterized as being beautiful and graceful. They are often depicted as having a youthful appearance, with long flowing hair and delicate features. They are often described as being playful, mischievous, and even flirtatious. Their beauty and charm have made them popular figures in literature and art, and they are often seen as symbols of fertility and abundance.

Nymphs are also known for their supernatural powers. They are often associated with healing, and they are believed to be able to grant wishes and influence the weather. They are also thought to be able to provide protection and guidance to those who seek it.

In terms of their place in the pantheon of mythical creatures, nymphs are often seen as being subordinate to gods and goddesses. They are often seen as messengers or servants of the gods, and they are sometimes seen as guardians of sacred places or objects. They are also sometimes seen as guides to the underworld, and they are sometimes associated with the dead.

Overall, nymphs are an important part of mythology and folklore, and they have been a source of fascination for centuries. They are associated with natural elements and they are known for their beauty and supernatural powers. They are also seen as being subordinate to gods and goddesses, and they are sometimes seen as guides to the underworld. They are an integral part of the pantheon of mythical creatures, and they provide an interesting glimpse into the mythology of the past.

2.

Killing a nymph is no easy task. Nymphs are supernatural creatures that inhabit the natural world and are considered to be immortal. They are known for their beauty, grace, and power, and are often seen as embodiments of nature and its elements. As such, they are highly revered and respected by many cultures and beliefs. So, how do you kill a nymph?

The answer to this question is not so straightforward. Nymphs are immortal, so it is impossible to kill them in the traditional sense. However, there are ways to incapacitate them and render them powerless. For example, some cultures believe that if a nymph is bound by a magical chain or rope, it will be rendered powerless and unable to use its powers. This is seen as a form of "killing" the nymph, as it is unable to use its powers or interact with the natural world.

In some cases, a nymph can be killed by magical means. For example, if a powerful spell is cast on the nymph, it can be killed. This is a difficult and dangerous task, however, as it requires great skill and knowledge of the magical arts. It is also important to note that the spell must be powerful enough to actually kill the nymph, which is not always easy to achieve.

In addition to magical means, some cultures believe that a nymph can be killed by physical means. For example, if a nymph is struck with a weapon made of silver, it can be killed. This is because silver is believed to have the power to harm and even kill supernatural creatures. It is important to note, however, that silver weapons are rare and difficult to come by, so this method is not always practical.

Finally, some cultures believe that a nymph can be killed by divine intervention. In this case, a powerful god or goddess must intervene and send a supernatural force to "kill" the nymph. This is an incredibly difficult task, as gods and goddesses are often difficult to summon and persuade. Furthermore, divine intervention is not always guaranteed, as gods and goddesses are not always willing to intervene in the affairs of mortals.

In conclusion, killing a nymph is not an easy task. Nymphs are immortal creatures, so it is impossible to kill them in the traditional sense. However, there are ways to incapacitate them and render them powerless, such as binding them with a magical chain or rope, casting powerful spells, or using silver weapons. In some cases, divine intervention may also be necessary. Ultimately, it is important to remember that killing a nymph is a difficult and dangerous task, and should not be taken lightly.

# Part 19

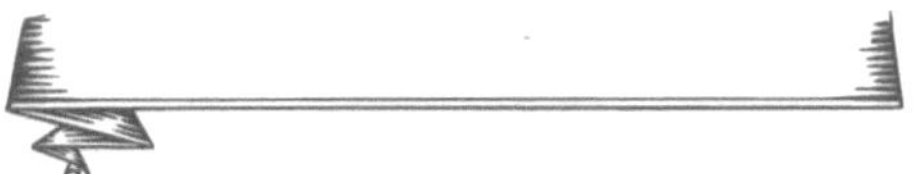

# Goblins

# Goblins
### 1.

A goblin is an otherworldly creature that has been a part of folklore and mythology for centuries. Generally, goblins are depicted as small, mischievous creatures with a penchant for causing chaos and mayhem. They are usually described as having green skin, pointy ears, and a large, bulbous nose. In many cultures, goblins are seen as a malicious force that should be avoided at all costs.

In medieval European folklore, goblins were typically seen as small, grotesque creatures that lived in the dark and damp places of the world. They were thought to be capable of stealing children, tormenting people, and generally causing destruction and chaos. They were also believed to be able to shape-shift, allowing them to take on the appearance of animals or humans in order to deceive their victims.

In some cultures, goblins were seen as helpful spirits. In some Native American tribes, goblins were seen as helpful spirits that could provide guidance and protection to those who asked for it. In Japan, goblins were seen as helpful spirits that could help guide people in the right direction.

Goblins have also been a part of popular culture for many years. In literature, goblins are often portrayed as mischievous creatures with a penchant for causing trouble. In the Harry Potter series, goblins were seen as a race of magical creatures that were capable of creating powerful magical artifacts. In the Lord of the Rings series, goblins were portrayed as a race of evil creatures that were enemies of the protagonists.

In modern popular culture, goblins are often portrayed as comic relief characters. They are often seen as bumbling and clumsy creatures that are more likely to cause trouble than actually help anyone. In the popular video game series The Elder Scrolls, goblins are seen as a race of mischievous creatures that are more likely to cause trouble than actually help anyone.

In conclusion, goblins are a creature that has been a part of folklore and mythology for centuries. They are typically seen as small, mischievous creatures with a penchant for causing chaos and mayhem. In some cultures, goblins are seen as helpful spirits, while in others they are seen as evil creatures to be avoided at all costs. In popular culture, goblins are often portrayed as comic relief characters that are more likely to cause trouble than actually help anyone.

2.

Killing a goblin is not an easy task, and there are many different methods that can be used to do so. The most important thing to remember when attempting to kill a goblin is to be prepared and to have the right tools and knowledge to do so. Depending on the type of goblin you are dealing with, different methods may be more effective than others.

The most common type of goblin is the small, green-skinned creature that is usually found in dungeons and caves. These goblins are usually not very strong and can be killed fairly easily with either a sword or a bow and arrow. If you are dealing with a larger goblin, however, it may be necessary to use more powerful weapons such as a mace or an axe. It is also important to remember that goblins have a natural affinity for magic and may be resistant to certain types of weapons, so it is important to research the type of goblin you are dealing with before attempting to kill it.

In addition to weapons, knowledge of the goblin's weaknesses can also be very helpful when attempting to kill one. For example, goblins are particularly vulnerable to fire and light, so if you have access to a torch or some other source of light, it can be used to your advantage. If you are dealing with a particularly powerful goblin, however, it may be necessary to use more powerful magic spells or potions to defeat it.

Another important factor to consider when trying to kill a goblin is the environment in which you are fighting it. If you are in a dungeon or cave, it may be more difficult to fight the goblin due to the enclosed space. If you are outdoors, however, you may have more room to maneuver and can use the terrain to your advantage.

Finally, it is important to remember that goblins are not the only creatures that can be found in dungeons and caves. There may be other monsters or creatures that could pose a threat to you, so it is important to be aware of your surroundings and be prepared for any potential danger.

In conclusion, killing a goblin is not an easy task, and it is important to be prepared and have the right tools and knowledge to do so. Different methods may be more effective depending on the type of goblin you are dealing with, and it is important to consider the environment in which you are fighting it. Knowing the goblin's weaknesses can also be very helpful, and it is important to remember that there may be other creatures in the area that could pose a threat to you. With the right preparation and knowledge, however, it is possible to successfully kill a goblin.

# Part 20

# Ogre

# Ogres
1.

An ogre is a large and often hideous creature found in many different mythologies and folklores around the world. It is typically described as a large, monstrous humanoid, often with green skin, a large head, and a voracious appetite. Ogres are known for their immense strength and their ability to cause destruction and chaos.

In many cultures, ogres are seen as evil creatures that feast on human flesh. They are often portrayed as living in caves, forests, or other remote places. Ogres are also known for their greed and their desire for power. They are often depicted as being violent and cruel, and they are often seen as the enemies of humans and other creatures.

Ogres have been a part of mythology and folklore since ancient times. In Greek mythology, ogres were known as the Cyclopes, a race of one-eyed giants. In Norse mythology, ogres were known as the jötnar, a race of giants who were enemies of the gods. In Hindu mythology, ogres were known as the rakshasas, a race of demonic creatures.

In modern popular culture, ogres are often portrayed as comedic characters. They are often depicted as being clumsy and bumbling, and they are often seen as being more of a nuisance than an actual threat. However, some modern interpretations of ogres still maintain their more sinister aspects, such as their strength and their willingness to cause destruction and chaos.

Ogres are also often associated with magic and sorcery. In some stories, ogres are portrayed as having magical powers, such as the ability to transform into different shapes or to control the elements. In other stories, ogres are seen as being powerful sorcerers who use their magic to cause destruction and chaos.

Overall, an ogre is a large and often hideous creature found in many different mythologies and folklores around the world. It is typically described as a large, monstrous humanoid, often with green skin, a large head, and a voracious appetite. Ogres are known for their immense strength and their ability to cause destruction and chaos. They are often seen as evil creatures that feast on human flesh, and they are often associated with magic and sorcery. In modern popular culture, ogres are often portrayed as comedic characters, but some modern interpretations of ogres still maintain their more sinister aspects.

2.

Killing an ogre can be a daunting task, especially for those who have never encountered one. Ogres are large, powerful creatures that can use their strength to overpower and defeat even the most experienced warriors. However, with the right knowledge and preparation, it is possible to take down an ogre and come out of the encounter alive.

The first step to killing an ogre is to understand the creature's strengths and weaknesses. Ogres are strong and resilient, but they are also slow and not particularly intelligent. They are also susceptible to certain weapons and spells, so it is important to know what weapons and spells will be effective against them. Additionally, ogres are often found in groups, so it is important to be prepared for multiple opponents.

Once the ogre's strengths and weaknesses are understood, the next step is to plan an attack strategy. It is important to be aware of the environment and to use it to one's advantage. For example, if the ogre is in an area with a lot of trees, then using ranged weapons such as bows and arrows can be effective. If the ogre is in an open area, then melee weapons such as swords and spears may be more effective. Additionally, it is important to have a plan for how to escape if the battle does not go as planned.

In addition to planning an attack strategy, it is also important to be prepared with the right equipment. Weapons such as swords, spears, and bows should be chosen based on the situation. Additionally, it is important to have healing potions and other items that can be used to restore health in case of injury. It is also important to be aware of the ogre's weaknesses and to be prepared with spells or items that can exploit them.

Finally, it is important to be confident and courageous in the face of an ogre. Ogres are intimidating creatures, but it is important to remember that they can be defeated. Having a plan and the right equipment can give one the confidence to face the ogre and come out of the encounter alive.

In conclusion, killing an ogre is a daunting task, but it is possible with the right knowledge and preparation. Understanding the ogre's strengths and weaknesses, planning an attack strategy, and being prepared with the right equipment are all important steps to take before facing an ogre. Additionally, it is important to remain confident and courageous in the face of the creature. With the right knowledge and preparation, it is possible to take down an ogre and come out of the encounter alive.

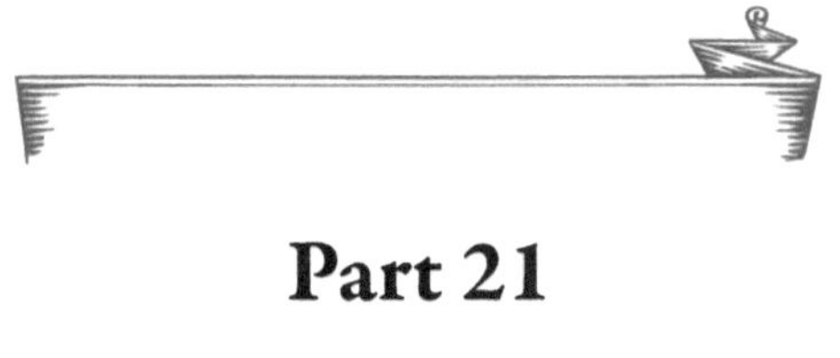

# Part 21

# Cyclops

# Cyclops
### 1.

Cyclops are a type of legendary creature found in Greek mythology. They are usually described as having a single eye in the center of their forehead, although some accounts describe them as having two eyes. Cyclopes are generally portrayed as strong and powerful beings, capable of performing great feats of strength.

The origin of the Cyclops is not clear, but they are believed to have originated in the Bronze Age. They were often associated with the god Poseidon, who was known to have a single eye in the middle of his forehead. In some accounts, the Cyclopes were the sons of Poseidon and the sea nymph Thoosa.

The most famous Cyclops in Greek mythology is Polyphemus, who appears in Homer's Odyssey. He is the son of Poseidon and Thoosa, and is described as being a giant with a single eye in the center of his forehead. He is known for trapping Odysseus and his crew in a cave, and eating some of them before being tricked by Odysseus and blinded.

In addition to Polyphemus, there are other Cyclopes in Greek mythology. These include Brontes, Steropes, and Arges, who were known as the "sons of Uranus" and were said to have been the builders of the walls of Troy. They were also said to be the creators of the thunderbolts of Zeus.

The Cyclopes were also associated with the Titans, a race of giant gods who were overthrown by the Olympian gods. The Cyclopes were said to have been the blacksmiths for the Titans, forging weapons and armor for them.

In some accounts, the Cyclopes were also said to be the builders of the Labyrinth of Crete, where the Minotaur was kept. They were also said to have been the builders of the walls of Mycenae.

Cyclopes are often depicted in works of art, especially in ancient Greek art. They are usually shown as large, muscular figures with a single eye in the center of their forehead. They are often shown holding a hammer or anvil, which is symbolic of their association with blacksmithing.

Cyclopes have also been featured in modern works of fiction, such as the X-Men comics and films, where they are portrayed as a race of mutants who possess superhuman strength and a single eye.

In conclusion, Cyclopes are an interesting and mysterious creature from Greek mythology. They are usually portrayed as strong and powerful beings, capable of performing great feats of strength. They are associated with the gods Poseidon and the Titans, and are often depicted in works of art. They have also been featured in modern works of fiction, such as the X-Men comics and films.

2.

Killing a cyclop is no easy feat. The cyclop, a mythical creature with one eye in the center of its forehead, is said to have immense strength and power. It is often depicted as a giant, fierce creature that is near impossible to defeat. The question of how to kill a cyclop has been debated for centuries, with many different theories and methods proposed. In this essay, I will explore some of the most popular methods for killing a cyclop and the pros and cons of each.

One of the most popular methods for killing a cyclop is to use a weapon. This could be anything from a sword to an arrow or even a gun. The advantage of this method is that it is relatively easy to do, and if done correctly, can be very effective. The disadvantage is that it requires the use of a weapon, which can be difficult to come by in some cases. Additionally, the cyclop may be too powerful for the weapon to be effective, or the weapon may not be able to penetrate its tough hide.

Another method for killing a cyclop is to use magic. This could include spells or charms that are designed to weaken the cyclop or even banish it from the area. The advantage of this method is that it does not require the use of a weapon and can be very effective. The disadvantage is that it requires knowledge of magic, which may not be available to everyone. Additionally, the cyclop may be too powerful for the magic to be effective.

A third method for killing a cyclop is to use a trap. This could include a pit or a snare that is designed to capture the cyclop and prevent it from escaping. The advantage of this method is that it requires no weapon and can be very effective. The disadvantage is that it requires knowledge of traps, which may not be available to everyone. Additionally, the cyclop may be too powerful for the trap to be effective.

Finally, there is the method of using brute force. This involves physically attacking the cyclop and trying to overpower it. The advantage of this method is that it does not require the use of a weapon or knowledge of traps or magic. The disadvantage is that it is very risky, as the cyclop is likely to be much stronger than the attacker. Additionally, the cyclop may be too powerful for the attacker to defeat.

In conclusion, killing a cyclop is no easy feat. There are several methods that can be used to do so, each with its own advantages and disadvantages. The best method for killing a cyclop will depend on the individual situation, so it is important to consider all the options before attempting to do so.

# Part 22

# Golems

# Golems
### 1.

A golem is a creature from Jewish folklore that is typically described as an artificially created being, usually made from clay or mud. The word "golem" has been used to refer to a variety of different types of creatures and entities, but it is most commonly associated with the idea of a humanoid figure that is brought to life through magical means. The concept of a golem has been around for centuries, with the earliest known references appearing in the Talmud, a collection of Jewish religious texts.

The most famous story of a golem comes from the 16th century, when a rabbi in Prague created a golem to protect the Jewish community from anti-Semitic attacks. The rabbi, Judah Loew ben Bezalel, created the golem from clay and brought it to life by writing the word "emeth" ("truth" in Hebrew) on its forehead. The golem was said to be an obedient and powerful servant, and it successfully defended the Jewish community from its attackers.

The concept of a golem has been used in literature and art throughout the centuries, with the most famous example being Mary Shelley's novel Frankenstein. In this classic work, the protagonist, Victor Frankenstein, creates a humanoid creature from parts of dead bodies and brings it to life using electricity. While Frankenstein's creature is not technically a golem, it has many similarities to the traditional golem, as it is an artificially created being that is brought to life through science instead of magic.

The idea of a golem has been used in many other works of literature and film over the years. For example, the Harry Potter series features a character named Dobby, who is a house-elf created by a witch. Dobby is similar to a golem in that he is a magical creature created to serve a master, although he is not made of clay or mud. In the Lord of the Rings series, the character of Golem is a giant construct made of stone and brought to life by a powerful wizard.

In modern times, the concept of a golem has been used to explore themes of artificial intelligence and robotics. In the 1982 film Blade Runner, a group of scientists create a golem-like creature known as a "replicant" that is designed to be indistinguishable from a human. The replicant is programmed with emotions and memories, and its creators struggle to control it and keep it from becoming too powerful.

The idea of a golem is also used in video games, such as the popular game series The Elder Scrolls. In this series, the player can create a golem-like creature known as a "construct" that is used to complete tasks and protect the player from harm.

Overall, a golem is a creature from Jewish folklore that is typically described as an artificially created being, usually made from clay or mud. The concept of a golem has been used in literature, film, and video games to explore themes of artificial intelligence and robotics. The most famous story of a golem comes from the 16th century, when a rabbi in Prague created a golem to protect the Jewish community from anti-Semitic attacks. The idea of a golem is still relevant today, as it is used to explore the implications of creating artificial life and the potential of technology to bring about powerful changes in the world.

2.

Killing a golem is no easy feat. This is because a golem is an artificial creature made out of inanimate matter, usually clay or mud, that is brought to life through magical means. Golems are usually created to serve a specific purpose and can be incredibly powerful and resilient. As such, it is not easy to simply destroy them. However, there are some methods that can be used to kill a golem.

The first and most obvious way to kill a golem is to destroy the source of its magic. This is usually done by removing or destroying the source of the golem's power, such as a magical amulet or a spellbook. Removing the source of the golem's power will cause it to become inert, and thus, it can easily be destroyed. However, this method is not always feasible, as the source of the golem's power may be difficult or impossible to find.

Another way to kill a golem is to use a powerful magical weapon. This could be a magical sword, staff, or even a powerful spell. The weapon or spell must be powerful enough to break the golem's magical defenses and cause it to become inert. However, this method is not always reliable, as the golem may be too powerful for the weapon or spell to be effective.

A third way to kill a golem is to use a powerful physical weapon. This could be a powerful weapon like a mace or hammer, or even a powerful spell. The physical weapon must be powerful enough to break through the golem's physical defenses and cause it to become inert. Again, this method is not always reliable, as the golem may be too powerful for the weapon or spell to be effective.

Finally, some golems can be killed by simply overpowering them. This is done by using a powerful magical or physical force to overwhelm the golem and cause it to become inert. This method is not always reliable, however, as the golem may be too powerful for the force to be effective.

In conclusion, killing a golem is no easy task. It requires a powerful magical or physical force to overpower it, or a powerful magical weapon or spell to break through its defenses. While these methods are not always reliable, they are the most effective ways to kill a golem.

# Part 23

# Witches

# Witches
### 1.

A witch is a person who practices witchcraft, a form of magic that is rooted in nature and the use of energy. Witches use their practice to bring about positive change in their lives and the lives of others. Witches are often associated with the occult and have been a part of folklore and mythology for centuries.

Witches are typically believed to be female, although male witches do exist. Witches often practice their craft alone, although there are covens of witches that practice together. They may use tools such as a cauldron, a broom, a wand, and candles, but these tools are not necessary to practice witchcraft.

The practice of witchcraft is often associated with the practice of spellcasting. Spells are a way of focusing energy and intent to bring about desired outcomes. Witches use their knowledge of herbs, crystals, and other natural elements to create spells. They may also use symbols and rituals to cast spells.

Witches may also practice divination, which is the practice of using tools such as tarot cards, runes, and pendulums to gain insight into the future. This practice is used to gain knowledge and understanding of events that may occur in the future.

Witches may also use rituals and ceremonies to honor the gods and goddesses of their faith. These rituals often involve the use of candles, incense, and other items that are believed to bring about positive change.

Witches are often seen as healers and are believed to be able to use their craft to bring about healing for physical, emotional, and spiritual ailments. Witches may use herbs, oils, and other natural elements to create healing potions and salves. They may also use spells and rituals to bring about healing.

Witches may also use their craft to protect themselves and those around them. They may use spells and rituals to create protective shields or to ward off negative energy.

The practice of witchcraft is often viewed as a form of empowerment and self-expression. Witches may use their craft to bring about positive change in their lives and the lives of those around them. Witches may also use their craft to explore their spirituality and to find a deeper connection to the divine.

In conclusion, a witch is a person who practices witchcraft, a form of magic that is rooted in nature and the use of energy. Witches use their practice to bring about positive change in their lives and the lives of others. They may use tools such as a cauldron, a broom, a wand, and candles, but these tools are not necessary to practice witchcraft. Witches may also practice divination, use spells and rituals to honor the gods and goddesses of their faith, and use their craft to bring about healing and protection. The practice of witchcraft is often viewed as a form of empowerment and self-expression.

2.

Killing an evil witch is no small feat. It requires a great deal of knowledge, courage, and strength of character. In this essay, I will discuss the steps necessary to successfully kill an evil witch.

The first step in killing an evil witch is to understand the nature of the witch and the power they possess. Witches are powerful beings who have access to dark magic and are capable of doing great harm. It is important to understand the extent of their power before attempting to take them on. Researching the witch's history and abilities is a crucial part of this process, as it will help you to understand the best way to approach the situation.

The second step is to prepare for the confrontation. This includes gathering the necessary supplies and allies to help in the fight. Weapons such as swords, crossbows, and magical items are all useful in taking down an evil witch. It is also important to enlist the help of others who are knowledgeable in the area of witchcraft, as they can provide valuable insight and assistance.

The third step is to confront the witch. This is not an easy task and requires a great deal of courage. It is important to be aware of the witch's abilities and to be prepared to defend oneself. It is also important to remember that witches are powerful and should not be underestimated.

The fourth step is to use the weapons and magical items that have been gathered to attack the witch. This is the most difficult part of the process and requires a great deal of skill and strategy. It is important to remember that the witch is powerful and should not be taken lightly.

The fifth and final step is to finish the witch off. This can be done in a variety of ways, depending on the situation. It is important to remember that the witch is powerful and should not be underestimated.

Killing an evil witch is no small feat and requires a great deal of knowledge, courage, and strength of character. It is important to be aware of the witch's abilities and to be prepared to defend oneself. It is also important to remember that witches are powerful and should not be underestimated. Gathering the necessary supplies and allies to help in the fight, confronting the witch, using the weapons and magical items to attack the witch, and finally finishing the witch off are all important steps in the process. With the right knowledge and preparation, it is possible to successfully kill an evil witch.

# Part 24

# shapeshifter

# Shapeshifter
1.

A shapeshifter is a creature found in many cultures across the world. It is a being that can take on the form of any creature or object, often with supernatural powers. Shapeshifters are usually seen as magical, mysterious, and sometimes dangerous entities.

In mythology, shapeshifters are often seen as gods or goddesses. Ancient Egyptians believed that the god Thoth could take the form of any animal or creature he chose. In Greek mythology, Proteus was a god of the sea who could take on any form he wanted. In Norse mythology, Odin was a shapeshifter who could take the form of animals, birds, and even humans.

Shapeshifters also appear in folklore and literature. In the Brothers Grimm fairy tale "The Frog Prince", the prince is transformed into a frog by an evil witch. In the Harry Potter series, Professor McGonagall can turn into a cat. In the Chronicles of Narnia, the White Witch can transform into a wolf.

Shapeshifters are often seen as powerful and dangerous creatures. In some cultures, they are seen as evil creatures that can take the form of humans and use their powers to deceive and harm people. In other cultures, shapeshifters are seen as wise and powerful beings who can help people in need.

Shapeshifting is a power that is often associated with witches and other magical beings. Witches are believed to be able to transform themselves into animals or other creatures, and use their powers to help or harm people. In some cultures, shapeshifting is seen as a form of witchcraft, and is believed to be a powerful form of magic.

Shapeshifting is also associated with shamanism. Shamans are believed to be able to take on the form of animals or other creatures, and use their powers to communicate with the spirit world. Shamans are believed to be able to transform into animals or other creatures in order to gain insight and knowledge.

Shapeshifting is a concept that has been around for centuries, and is still popular in many cultures today. It is seen as a powerful form of magic that can be used for both good and evil. It is a concept that is often used in literature and film, and is a popular topic of discussion among those who are interested in mythology and folklore.

2.

These elusive creatures possess the ability to transform their physical form into any living creature they desire, making them nearly impossible to track down. As a result, it can be quite difficult to determine how to go about killing a shapeshifter. However, with the right knowledge and preparation, it is possible to successfully take down one of these elusive creatures.

The first step in killing a shapeshifter is to identify the creature and its true form. Shapeshifters are known to take on the form of animals, humans, and even mythical creatures. It is important to be able to recognize the shapeshifter in its true form so that you can properly prepare for the battle ahead. In some cases, shapeshifters may be able to disguise themselves as a different creature in order to throw off their pursuers. If this is the case, it is important to be on the lookout for any strange behavior or changes in the creature's appearance that may indicate a shapeshifter is present.

Once the shapeshifter's true form is identified, the next step is to prepare for the battle. It is important to arm yourself with weapons that are capable of penetrating the shapeshifter's thick skin. Silver and iron are two of the most effective materials for this purpose, as they are known to be effective against shapeshifters. It is also important to be aware of the shapeshifter's weaknesses, which may include sunlight, water, and certain herbs and plants. Knowing the creature's weaknesses will give you an advantage in the battle.

Once you are adequately prepared, the next step is to engage the shapeshifter in battle. It is important to be aware that shapeshifters are often extremely powerful and dangerous creatures. As such, it is important to be prepared for a lengthy and difficult battle. During the battle, it is important to stay focused and to not give in to fear or panic. It is also important to remember that the shapeshifter may be able to transform into another creature, so it is important to stay on your guard.

Finally, once the battle is won, the last step is to ensure that the shapeshifter is completely dead. This can be done by burning the body or burying it in consecrated ground. It is important to remember that shapeshifters can regenerate and come back to life, so it is important to take the necessary precautions to ensure that the creature does not return.

Killing a shapeshifter is no easy task, but with the right knowledge and preparation, it is possible to successfully take down one of these elusive creatures. By identifying the shapeshifter's true form, arming yourself with the proper weapons, engaging in battle, and taking the necessary precautions to ensure the creature is dead, you can successfully kill a shapeshifter and protect yourself and those around you from harm.

# Part 25

# Demons

# Demons

### 1.

When it comes to the concept of a demon, there is no one definitive answer. Depending on the culture and context, the definition of a demon can vary greatly. Generally, however, a demon is an evil spirit, usually with supernatural powers, that is believed to cause harm and chaos. In some cases, demons are seen as the cause of physical and mental illness, while in others, they are seen as the bringers of misfortune and bad luck.

The concept of a demon has been around for thousands of years, with references to them in ancient texts and cultures. In the Bible, for example, demons are mentioned numerous times, often as evil forces. Ancient Greeks and Romans also saw demons as evil forces, with the god Apollo being thought to have the power to cast out demons. In Chinese culture, demons were seen as evil spirits that could be appeased with offerings and sacrifices.

In many cultures, demons are seen as a representation of evil, darkness, and chaos. They are often associated with sin and temptation, and are thought to be the source of all evil in the world. Demons are also often seen as the cause of physical and mental illness, as well as misfortune and bad luck. In some cases, they are even thought to possess people and influence their actions.

In modern times, the concept of a demon has become more complex. While traditional beliefs still hold true in some cases, many people now view demons as a metaphor for the inner struggles and difficulties we face in life. In this sense, demons can represent the inner darkness and chaos that can arise from our own thoughts and emotions. They can also be seen as a representation of the destructive forces that exist within us, such as fear, guilt, and anger.

The concept of a demon is a complex one, and there is no one definitive answer. Depending on the culture and context, the definition of a demon can vary greatly. Generally, however, a demon is an evil spirit, usually with supernatural powers, that is believed to cause harm and chaos. In some cases, demons are seen as the cause of physical and mental illness, while in others, they are seen as the bringers of misfortune and bad luck. No matter how one views them, it is clear that demons have been an important part of human culture for thousands of years, and will continue to be so for many more.

2.

Killing a demon is no easy task. It requires a great deal of knowledge and skill, as well as courage and determination. One must understand the true nature of a demon in order to effectively combat it. Demons are supernatural entities that exist in many cultures and religions, often associated with evil and chaos. They are powerful and dangerous, and should not be taken lightly.

The first step in killing a demon is to gain knowledge about it. Researching the demon's history, origin, and behavior is essential in order to understand its weaknesses and how to best combat it. Knowing the demon's strengths and weaknesses is also important, as it will allow one to craft a strategy for defeating it. Additionally, it is important to understand the demon's motivations and goals, as this can be used to one's advantage.

Once one has gained an understanding of the demon's nature, the next step is to prepare for battle. This may include gathering the necessary weapons and supplies, such as holy water, blessed objects, and other items that can be used to ward off the demon. It is also important to enlist the help of allies, such as priests, shamans, or other people who have experience in dealing with the supernatural.

The final step is to confront the demon. This is the most dangerous part of the process, and should not be taken lightly. It is important to remember that demons are powerful and dangerous, and should not be underestimated. It is also important to keep in mind that the demon may have allies or minions that must be dealt with as well.

When confronting the demon, it is important to stay focused and maintain one's composure. It is also important to remember that the demon is an entity of chaos, and should be treated with respect. It is important to remain calm and not act rashly, as this could lead to disaster.

Once the demon has been confronted, it is important to be prepared to finish it off. Depending on the type of demon, this may involve using a variety of methods, such as holy water, blessed objects, or other methods of banishing or binding the demon. It is also important to ensure that the demon is completely destroyed, as leaving even a fragment of it can result in it returning and causing further chaos.

Killing a demon is no easy task, and requires great skill and knowledge. It is important to remember that demons are powerful and dangerous, and should not be taken lightly. By researching the demon's history and behavior, preparing for battle, and confronting the demon with courage and determination, one can successfully defeat it.

# Part 25

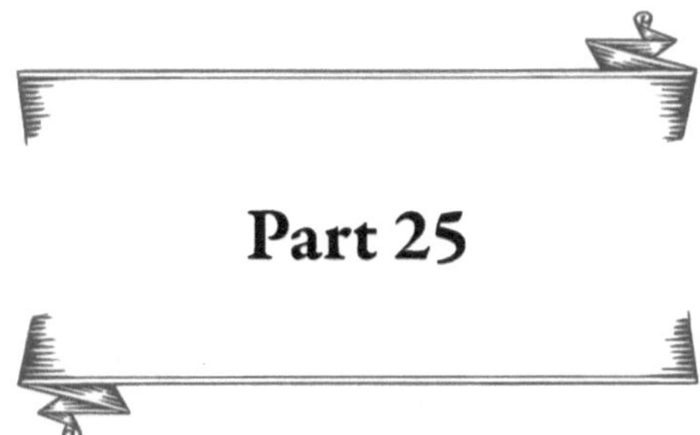

# Djinn

# D<sup>jinn</sup> 1.

A Djinn is an ancient supernatural being found in many different cultures throughout history. They are often described as powerful, mysterious, and magical creatures that can grant wishes. Djinns can be both benevolent and malevolent, depending on the context and situation. In some cultures, they are seen as gods or spirits, while in others they are seen as demons or evil forces.

The origin of the Djinn is uncertain, but they are believed to have originated in the Middle East and the Arabian Peninsula. The word Djinn is derived from the Arabic term jinn, which means "spirit" or "hidden." The Djinn are mentioned in the Qur'an and Islamic mythology, as well as in other ancient texts such as the Babylonian Talmud and the Torah.

The Djinn are often depicted as anthropomorphic creatures with human-like features. They are usually depicted as having wings, and can take on a variety of forms including humans, animals, and objects. They are also known to possess magical powers such as invisibility, shape-shifting, and the ability to grant wishes.

The Djinn are believed to be able to interact with humans, and are sometimes associated with good luck or fortune. They can be invoked through incantations and rituals, and are believed to be able to grant wishes or provide guidance. They are also believed to be able to possess humans, and can be used to manipulate or control people.

In some cultures, the Djinn are believed to be able to control the weather and natural disasters. They are also believed to be able to cause illness or misfortune. In some cases, they are believed to be able to bring wealth and abundance to those who invoke them.

The Djinn are often associated with the occult and superstition, and are believed to be able to influence people's lives in both positive and negative ways. They are often used in various forms of divination, such as tarot readings, and are believed to be able to provide insight into the future.

Despite their mysterious and often feared nature, the Djinn are still seen as powerful and benevolent forces in many cultures. They are believed to be able to help those who invoke them, and can provide protection and guidance when called upon. They are also believed to be able to bring good luck, wealth, and prosperity to those who invoke them.

In conclusion, the Djinn are an ancient supernatural being found in many different cultures throughout history. They are often depicted as powerful, mysterious, and magical creatures that can grant wishes. They are believed to be able to interact with humans, and are sometimes associated with good luck or fortune. Despite their mysterious and often feared nature, the Djinn are still seen as powerful and benevolent forces in many cultures, and are believed to be able to help those who invoke them.

2.

For centuries, people have wondered how to kill a Djinn, and while there is no definitive answer, there are some methods that have been used in the past.

The most common way to kill a Djinn is by using a magical weapon. These weapons can be anything from a sword to a bow and arrow, depending on the type of Djinn. In some cases, a magical weapon may be needed to even have a chance at killing a Djinn. For example, in the Arabian Nights, King Solomon was able to control the Djinn with his magical ring.

Another method of killing a Djinn is by using a powerful incantation. Incantations can be used to weaken a Djinn and make them vulnerable to attack. The incantation must be spoken with precision and power in order to be effective. In some cases, the incantation must be spoken in a specific language, such as Arabic or Hebrew.

In addition to magical weapons and incantations, there are also certain rituals that can be used to kill a Djinn. These rituals can involve burning certain herbs, reciting certain prayers, and using specific objects. For example, in some traditions, a person can use a magical knife to cut off the head of a Djinn. This is believed to be the only way to truly kill a Djinn.

Finally, it is important to remember that the Djinn can also be killed by the power of faith. Belief in a higher power and faith in the divine can be used to weaken a Djinn and make them vulnerable to attack. This is often done through prayer and meditation.

No matter which method is used, it is important to remember that killing a Djinn is a dangerous and difficult task. It requires a great deal of preparation and knowledge, and should only be attempted by those who are experienced in dealing with the supernatural. It is also important to remember that killing a Djinn will not always be successful, and could have unforeseen consequences.

In conclusion, killing a Djinn is a difficult task that requires knowledge, preparation, and faith. The most common methods of killing a Djinn include using a magical weapon, reciting an incantation, performing a ritual, or relying on the power of faith. It is important to remember that killing a Djinn is a dangerous task, and should only be attempted by those who are experienced in dealing with the supernatural.

# Part 26

# Wendigo

# Wendigo

### 1.

A wendigo is a mythical creature that has been featured in the folklore of Native American tribes, particularly those located in the northern parts of the United States and Canada. It is a malevolent, cannibalistic spirit that is said to possess great strength and the ability to transform into a giant, monstrous beast. The wendigo is often described as having a human body with a wolf-like head, long claws, and glowing, red eyes.

Though the wendigo has been a part of Native American folklore for centuries, the concept of the creature has become increasingly popular in recent years due to its inclusion in popular culture. The wendigo has been featured in books, movies, television shows, and video games, and has been used as a symbol of evil and darkness.

The origin of the wendigo is somewhat unclear, though it is believed to have originated with the Algonquin people of North America. According to Algonquin mythology, the wendigo was an evil spirit that could possess humans and turn them into cannibalistic monsters. It was believed that those who consumed human flesh would become cursed and transformed into a wendigo, and it was believed that only powerful medicine men could break the curse.

The wendigo is often associated with winter and cold weather, and is believed to be a spirit of starvation and death. It was believed that the wendigo would haunt those who were lost in the wilderness and would lead them to their deaths. It was also believed that the wendigo could take control of a person's mind, and would force them to commit acts of cannibalism.

Though the wendigo has been a part of Native American folklore for centuries, it has become increasingly popular in recent years due to its inclusion in popular culture. The wendigo has been featured in books, movies, television shows, and video games, and has been used as a symbol of evil and darkness. It is often depicted as a powerful and terrifying creature, and is often used as a metaphor for the dark side of human nature.

The wendigo has become a popular symbol of horror, and is often used in horror films and literature to represent the dark side of human nature. Though the wendigo is often depicted as an evil and terrifying creature, it is also seen as a symbol of strength and power. It is believed that those who confront the wendigo and survive its wrath will gain strength and courage, and will be able to overcome their fears.

In conclusion, the wendigo is a mythical creature that has been featured in the folklore of Native American tribes, particularly those located in the northern parts of the United States and Canada. It is a malevolent, cannibalistic spirit that is said to possess great strength and the ability to transform into a giant, monstrous beast. The wendigo has become increasingly popular in recent years due to its inclusion in popular culture, and is often used as a symbol of evil and darkness. It is also seen as a symbol of strength and power, and is believed that those who confront the wendigo and survive its wrath will gain strength and courage.

# Part 27

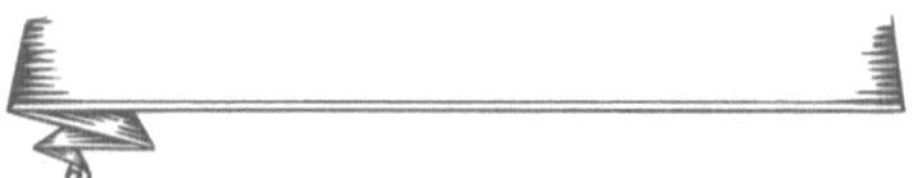

# Changeling

# Changeling

### 1.

A changeling is a creature in folklore that is exchanged for a human baby in a superstitious practice. It is believed that fairies, trolls, and other supernatural creatures would take a human baby from its parents and leave one of their own in its place. This creature was known as a changeling and was believed to possess magical powers.

The concept of the changeling dates back to ancient mythology, with stories of the substitution of a divine being for a human child. In the Greek myth of Zeus and Leda, Zeus transformed himself into a swan and replaced Leda's baby with a divine one. In the Norse myth of Odin and Rind, Odin took Rind's baby and left a changeling in its place.

The changeling was believed to be a mischievous creature that could cause havoc in the household. It was thought that the changeling would bring misfortune, disease, and even death to the family. To protect against the changeling's curse, people would often take certain precautions, such as keeping a fire burning in the house or placing a hot iron near the baby's crib.

In some cases, the changeling was believed to be a fairy child that had been stolen from its parents and left in the human world. These changelings were said to have magical powers, such as the ability to grant wishes or to cause mischief. It was also believed that the changeling could be returned to its fairy parents if certain conditions were met.

Changelings have been featured in literature and film, often as a source of fear and mystery. In the Brothers Grimm tale of Hansel and Gretel, the witch is said to have taken Hansel and left a changeling in his place. In the Harry Potter series, the character of Professor Dumbledore is revealed to be a changeling. In the horror film The Changeling, a ghostly changeling takes the place of a young boy who has gone missing.

The concept of the changeling is still present in some cultures today. In Ireland, for example, it is believed that fairies can steal babies and replace them with changelings. In some cases, the family will try to get the original baby back by giving the changeling a gift or performing a ritual.

In conclusion, a changeling is a creature from folklore that is exchanged for a human baby in a superstitious practice. It is believed to be a mischievous creature with magical powers that can bring misfortune and disease to a family. Changelings have been featured in literature and film, often as a source of fear and mystery. The concept of the changeling is still present in some cultures today, with families trying to get the original baby back by giving the changeling a gift or performing a ritual.

2.

Killing a changeling is no easy feat. Changelings are mythical creatures that can take on the form of any living being, and they are often said to be able to shapeshift into animals, humans, and even inanimate objects. This makes them incredibly difficult to track down and kill, as they can easily disguise themselves in plain sight. As such, there are a few methods that have been used over the years to try and kill a changeling.

The first method is to use a silver knife or blade. Silver is considered to be a powerful weapon against changelings, as it is believed to be able to penetrate their magical defenses and cause them harm. It is also said to be able to cut through their shapeshifting abilities and force them to take on their true form. If a silver blade is used, it is important to remember to use it quickly and decisively, as the changeling may be able to escape if given the chance.

The second method is to use a magical charm or spell. There are a variety of charms and spells that are said to be effective against changelings, such as charms that can bind them and prevent them from shapeshifting, or spells that can weaken them and make them vulnerable. It is important to be careful when using these charms and spells, as they can be dangerous and unpredictable.

The third method is to use a magical potion. There are a variety of potions that are said to be effective against changelings, such as potions that can weaken them, or potions that can force them to take on their true form. It is important to remember to use the potion quickly and decisively, as the changeling may be able to escape if given the chance.

The fourth method is to use a magical trap. Traps can be used to capture a changeling and prevent it from escaping. These traps often involve using items such as mirrors, crystals, or other objects that are believed to be able to trap the changeling's essence. Once the changeling is trapped, it can then be killed.

Finally, the fifth method is to use a magical weapon. Magical weapons are said to be able to penetrate the changeling's magical defenses and cause them harm. These weapons can be anything from swords to staffs, and they often require special rituals or spells to be used in order to be effective.

These are just a few of the methods that can be used to kill a changeling. It is important to remember to use caution when attempting to kill one, as they can be powerful and unpredictable. It is also important to remember that each changeling is unique, and what works for one may not work for another. It is best to consult an expert before attempting to kill a changeling, as they will be able to provide advice and guidance on the best methods to use.

# Part 28

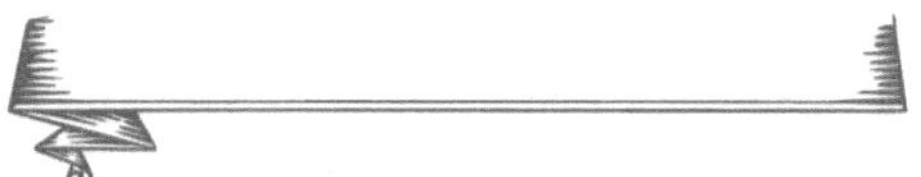

# Rugaru

# Rugaru
### 1.

A Rugaru is an ancient creature of folklore that has been discussed in various cultures for centuries. Originating from the Native American Algonquin culture, the Rugaru is a humanoid creature that is often described as having a wolf-like head and long, shaggy fur. It is said to be a dangerous beast, capable of attacking and devouring humans.

The Rugaru has been mentioned in various works of literature, including the famous Native American legend of the Wendigo. According to the legend, the Rugaru is a cannibalistic creature that preys on humans and is said to be an omen of death and destruction. It is believed that the Rugaru is a spirit that is summoned by witches and can be commanded to do their bidding.

The Rugaru is also featured in some horror movies, such as the movie "Jeepers Creepers". In this movie, the Rugaru is depicted as a monster that preys on humans and feeds on their flesh. It is said to possess supernatural powers, such as the ability to transform into a wolf or other animal.

The Rugaru is also mentioned in some religious texts, such as the Bible. In the Bible, the Rugaru is described as a creature of evil and is said to be the embodiment of Satan. It is believed that the Rugaru is a powerful spirit that is capable of causing great destruction and death.

In modern times, the Rugaru is still a popular subject in folklore and mythology. It is often used as a symbol of evil and is sometimes used as a metaphor for the power of evil in the world. It is believed that the Rugaru is a powerful force that can be used to cause harm and destruction.

Despite its sinister reputation, the Rugaru is not always seen as a malevolent creature. In some cultures, the Rugaru is seen as a protector and guardian of the people. It is said to be a powerful spirit that can be summoned to protect and aid those in need.

Overall, the Rugaru is an interesting creature of folklore that has been discussed in various cultures for centuries. It is a powerful creature that is capable of causing great destruction and death, yet it can also be seen as a protector and guardian of the people. It is a fascinating creature that is still discussed in modern times and is sure to continue to fascinate people for centuries to come.

2.

The first thing to consider when trying to kill a Rugaru is to understand what it is and what it is capable of. There are many stories and legends that have been passed down from generation to generation about the Rugaru, but they all have one thing in common: the Rugaru is a formidable and dangerous creature. It is said to be able to run at incredible speeds and is incredibly strong. It also has sharp claws and teeth that can easily tear through flesh.

The second thing to consider when trying to kill a Rugaru is to understand what weapons and tactics are necessary. The Rugaru is a creature of myth and legend, and it is not something that can be taken lightly. It is said that the only way to kill a Rugaru is to make sure that it is completely destroyed. This means that using weapons such as swords, spears, arrows, and even guns may not be enough to take down a Rugaru. It is said that the only way to kill a Rugaru is to use fire.

The third thing to consider when trying to kill a Rugaru is to understand the risks involved. Fire is a powerful weapon, and it can be dangerous if not used properly. It is important to make sure that the area is clear of any flammable material and that the fire is contained. It is also important to make sure that the fire is not too big or too small, as either situation can be dangerous. It is also important to make sure that the fire is not too close to the Rugaru, as it may be able to escape the flames.

The fourth thing to consider when trying to kill a Rugaru is to understand the importance of timing. It is important to make sure that the fire is used at the right time. If the fire is used too early, the Rugaru may be able to escape the flames. If the fire is used too late, the Rugaru may be able to recover and attack again. It is important to make sure that the fire is used at the right time in order to ensure that the Rugaru is destroyed.

Finally, it is important to understand the importance of preparation. It is important to make sure that all of the necessary supplies are gathered before attempting to kill a Rugaru. This includes things such as fuel, matches, and a way to contain the fire. It is also important to make sure that the area is clear of any flammable material and that the fire is contained.

Killing a Rugaru is no easy task, and it is something that should not be taken lightly. It is important to understand what the Rugaru is and what it is capable of, as well as the weapons and tactics necessary to take it down. It is also important to understand the risks involved, as well as the importance of timing and preparation. With the proper knowledge and preparation, killing a Rugaru can be done, but it is something that should not be taken lightly.

# Part 29

# Arachne

# Arachne

### 1.

An arachne is a type of mythological creature that has been featured in stories since ancient times. It is a hybrid of a spider and a human, and it is often portrayed as a dangerous creature that can spin webs and capture its prey. In Greek mythology, Arachne was a mortal woman who was so skilled at weaving that she challenged Athena, the goddess of wisdom and crafts, to a weaving contest. When Athena discovered that Arachne had woven a tapestry that was more beautiful than her own, she was so enraged that she turned Arachne into a spider.

The arachne is often seen as a symbol of female power and creativity. In some stories, the arachne is a villainous creature that is feared and avoided, while in others it is a helpful creature that helps humans in need. In some stories, the arachne is a creature of great wisdom and knowledge that can help humans understand the mysteries of the universe.

The arachne is a creature with many different aspects. It is often seen as a symbol of female power and creativity, but it can also represent danger and fear. The arachne is often portrayed as a creature of great wisdom and knowledge, and it is sometimes seen as a helpful creature that can assist humans in need.

The arachne is a creature with many different powers. It is often seen as a creature that can spin webs and capture its prey, but it also has the ability to create illusions and to transform into other creatures. In some stories, the arachne is a creature of great wisdom and knowledge that can help humans understand the mysteries of the universe.

The arachne is a creature that has been featured in many different stories throughout the ages. In some stories, it is a villainous creature that is feared and avoided, while in others it is a helpful creature that can help humans in need. It is a creature with many different aspects, and it is often seen as a symbol of female power and creativity. The arachne is a creature with many different powers, and it is a creature that has been featured in stories since ancient times.

2.

Killing an arachne is no easy task. As mythological creatures, arachnes are incredibly powerful and resilient, making them difficult to defeat. As a result, it is important to understand the unique characteristics of arachnes and how to use them to your advantage when trying to kill one.

An arachne is a mythological creature with the upper body of a human and the lower body of a spider. They are said to have been created by the goddess Athena, who was angered by the hubris of Arachne, a mortal woman who boasted of her weaving skills. As punishment, Athena transformed Arachne into a being with the lower body of a spider.

Arachnes have a variety of unique abilities. They are incredibly agile and can move quickly in any direction. They also have powerful venom which can paralyze their victims. Additionally, they can use their webs to ensnare their prey and immobilize them.

In order to kill an arachne, it is important to first understand their weaknesses. Arachnes are vulnerable to fire and bright light, as it can disrupt their webs and make them easier to defeat. Additionally, they are vulnerable to weapons made of silver, as it can pierce their tough exoskeleton and cause severe damage.

Once you have identified the weaknesses of an arachne, it is important to use them to your advantage. One way to do this is to use fire to disrupt their webs and make them easier to attack.

Additionally, weapons made of silver can be used to pierce their exoskeleton and cause severe damage. It is also important to wear protective clothing when fighting an arachne, as their venom can be extremely dangerous.

Finally, it is important to remember that arachnes are incredibly powerful and resilient creatures. As a result, it is important to be prepared and have a plan before attempting to kill one. It is also important to remain calm and focused in the face of danger, as this can help you stay on top of the situation and make the most of the situation.

In conclusion, killing an arachne is no easy task. However, with the right preparation and understanding of their weaknesses, it is possible to defeat them. It is important to remember that arachnes are incredibly powerful and resilient creatures, so it is important to be prepared and have a plan before attempting to kill one. Additionally, it is important to use their weaknesses to your advantage and wear protective clothing to protect yourself from their venom. By following these steps, you can successfully kill an arachne and protect yourself from harm.

# Part 30

# Hellhound

# Hellhound

1.

A Hellhound is a supernatural creature that is often featured in folklore. It is typically described as a large, black dog with glowing red eyes that is often associated with the underworld and the afterlife. It is believed that these creatures are sent from the afterlife to guard the entrance to the underworld and to hunt down those who have escaped from their punishment.

The origin of the Hellhound is unknown, but it is believed that they have been around since ancient times. In some cultures, they are seen as a symbol of death and destruction, while in others they are seen as a protective force. Whatever their origin, these creatures have been feared by many throughout the centuries.

In mythology, Hellhounds are often associated with the Greek god Hades. He is said to have used them to guard the entrance to the underworld and to hunt down those who have escaped from their punishment. In some stories, they are also said to be able to see and hear what is happening on the other side of the underworld, allowing them to keep watch over the souls of the dead.

In some cultures, Hellhounds are seen as a sign of bad luck and are believed to bring misfortune to anyone who encounters them. In some cases, they may even be seen as a sign of impending death. In other cultures, they are seen as a force of protection, guarding the entrance to the underworld and keeping the dead safe from harm.

In popular culture, Hellhounds have been featured in many books, movies, and television shows. They are often seen as a symbol of evil and are often used as a plot device to create suspense and fear. They are also used as a metaphor for the consequences of one's actions, as they are often sent to hunt down those who have escaped from their punishment.

No matter how they are portrayed, Hellhounds remain a popular figure in folklore and popular culture. They are a powerful symbol of death and destruction, and they can be used to create suspense and fear in stories and films. They are also a reminder that there are consequences to our actions, and that we should be careful not to cross the line.

2.

Killing a hellhound is no easy feat. As supernatural creatures born from the depths of the underworld, these beasts have been known to be virtually indestructible and able to withstand even the most powerful of weapons. But, despite their formidable reputation, there are ways to kill a hellhound.

The first step in killing a hellhound is to understand their weaknesses. Hellhounds are most vulnerable to the forces of light and dark magic. Light magic can be used to weaken the hellhound's defenses, while dark magic can be used to outright kill it. It is important to note that both forms of magic must be used together in order to be effective.

Once the hellhound has been weakened by the powers of light and dark magic, the next step is to use a weapon. The most effective weapon against a hellhound is a special type of enchanted blade that has been imbued with powerful magical properties. This blade must be forged from the strongest of metals and blessed with the power of the gods in order to be effective.

Once the blade has been forged, the next step is to confront the hellhound. This is not an easy task, as hellhounds are incredibly powerful and dangerous creatures. It is important to be prepared for battle and to have a plan in place before engaging the beast.

When the time comes to strike, the enchanted blade must be used to pierce the hellhound's heart. This is the only way to ensure that the hellhound is killed. If the blade is not strong enough, the hellhound will simply be weakened and will be able to recover.

Once the hellhound has been killed, it is important to remember to dispose of the body properly. Hellhounds are powerful creatures and their bodies can still contain powerful magical properties even after death. It is important to bury the body in consecrated ground or to burn it to ensure that no one can use the corpse for nefarious purposes.

Killing a hellhound is no easy task. It requires a great deal of preparation and knowledge in order to be successful. But, with the right tools and knowledge, it is possible to defeat these powerful creatures. With the right preparation and a strong weapon, it is possible to take down a hellhound and end its reign of terror.

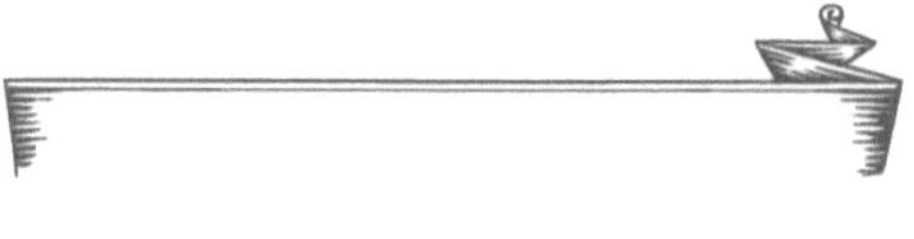

# Part 31

# Ghoul

# Ghoul

1.

A ghoul is a creature of folklore and mythology that is believed to haunt graveyards and feed on corpses. It is also sometimes referred to as a "ghoule" or "ghul". The term is derived from the Arabic word "ghul", which means "demon". Ghouls are typically depicted as humanoid creatures with an insatiable appetite for human flesh.

Ghouls have been a part of folklore and mythology for centuries, and stories of them have been told all over the world. In some cultures, they are seen as evil, while in others, they are seen as mischievous spirits. In some stories, they are seen as helpful creatures who will protect graves and guard them from desecration.

The exact origins of the ghoul are unknown, but they are believed to have originated in Mesopotamian mythology. In the Epic of Gilgamesh, a ghoul is described as a creature that lives in the desert and feeds on corpses. This is one of the earliest written accounts of ghouls and it is believed that the concept of ghouls originated in this region.

In some versions of the story, ghouls are described as having the power to shape-shift into animals, and they are often associated with the night and the dead. They are also believed to have the ability to possess humans and influence their behavior. In many stories, they are seen as a sign of impending danger or death.

Ghouls are often described as having a variety of supernatural powers, such as the ability to fly, turn invisible, and even control the minds of their victims. They are also believed to be able to communicate with the dead and are said to be able to foretell the future.

In some cultures, ghouls are seen as a protective force, while in others, they are seen as an evil force. In some cultures, they are seen as helpful creatures who can provide guidance and advice. In others, they are seen as malevolent creatures who are out to cause harm.

In most stories, ghouls are depicted as living in graveyards and feeding on corpses. They are typically described as being tall and thin, with pale skin, long claws, and a sharp beak. They are typically portrayed as having a grotesque appearance, with tattered clothing and a menacing gaze.

Ghouls are often seen as a threat to humans, but they are also seen as a source of protection. In some cultures, ghouls are seen as a sign of impending danger and are believed to be able to protect graves from desecration. In other cultures, they are seen as helpful creatures who can provide guidance and advice.

Overall, ghouls are a fascinating creature of folklore and mythology that has been around for centuries. They are typically seen as a source of fear and danger, but in some cultures, they are seen as a source of protection and guidance. The exact origins of the ghoul are unknown, but it is believed to have originated in Mesopotamian mythology. No matter how they are viewed, ghouls remain a fascinating creature in folklore and mythology.

2.

Killing a ghoul is no easy task, but it can be done with the right preparation and knowledge. Ghouls are creatures that have been around for centuries, and while they are often feared, they can be defeated with the right strategy. In order to successfully kill a ghoul, it is important to understand what they are, how they move, and what weapons are most effective against them.

Ghouls are undead creatures that are usually described as having a humanoid shape and often have a rotting or skeletal appearance. They are typically found in dark places such as graveyards and crypts, and they feed on the flesh of the living. They are also known to possess supernatural powers such as the ability to turn invisible or to control the minds of those around them.

Ghouls move quickly and can be difficult to catch, so it is important to be prepared before attempting to kill one. It is best to arm yourself with a weapon that is effective against them, such as a silver sword, a crossbow, or a stake. Silver is particularly effective against ghouls because it is believed to be able to disrupt their supernatural powers. It is also important to be aware of the environment you are in and to have a plan of escape in case the ghoul proves to be too powerful.

Once you have your weapon and you are prepared to face the ghoul, it is important to remember that they are vulnerable to sunlight. If you can lure the ghoul out into the open during the day, it will weaken them and make it easier to defeat them. If you are unable to lure them out, then you must be prepared to fight them in the dark. In this case, it is important to have a light source so that you can see the ghoul and attack it.

When attacking the ghoul, it is important to remember that they are resistant to physical damage. You must be prepared to use your weapon to its fullest potential in order to defeat the ghoul. Aim for the head or heart if possible, as these are the most vulnerable areas. If you are using a crossbow or stake, make sure to aim for the heart or head as these will be the most effective.

Once you have successfully killed the ghoul, it is important to remember to dispose of the body properly. Ghouls are believed to be able to come back from the dead, so it is important to make sure that the body is completely destroyed. Burning the body is the most effective way to ensure that the ghoul will not come back.

Killing a ghoul can be a difficult and dangerous task, but with the right preparation and knowledge it can be done. It is important to arm yourself with the right weapons, to be aware of the environment, and to have a plan of escape. It is also important to remember that ghouls are vulnerable to sunlight and that they are resistant to physical damage. Finally, once the ghoul is defeated, it is important to dispose of the body properly in order to ensure that it will not come back. With the right strategy, killing a ghoul is possible.

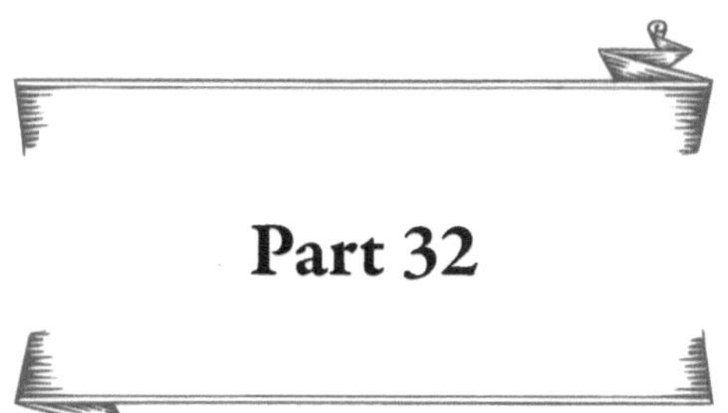

# Part 32

# Shtriga

# Shtriga
### 1.

A shtriga is a type of witch found in Albanian folklore. It is an evil creature that is believed to feed on the life force of young children, usually while they sleep. Shtrigas are usually female, though some stories describe them as male. They are said to be able to transform into a variety of different animals, such as a bee, a moth, or a fly.

The shtriga is believed to be a supernatural being, with the ability to fly, and to possess great strength. They are said to be able to control the weather, and to cause illness or death by draining the life force from their victims. They are also said to be able to shape-shift, and to have the ability to turn invisible.

In some stories, the shtriga is described as a beautiful woman who lures young men to their deaths, or as a hag who is always accompanied by a black cat. In other stories, the shtriga is described as an old woman who lives in the forest and preys on young children.

Shtrigas are most commonly found in Albania, though they are also found in other parts of the Balkans and in parts of Italy. In Albania, they are believed to be particularly active during the summer months, when they are said to be able to fly freely and to feed on the life force of children.

In order to protect children from the shtriga, there are a number of traditional methods that are used. One of the most common is to place a piece of iron, such as a nail, in a baby's crib. This is believed to protect the child from the shtriga's evil influence. Other methods include placing a cross on the child's forehead, or placing a red ribbon around the child's neck.

The shtriga is a figure that is deeply embedded in Albanian folklore, and has been the subject of many stories and legends. In some stories, the shtriga is seen as a helpful figure, who can be called upon to bring good luck and fortune. In other stories, the shtriga is seen as a dangerous creature, who must be avoided at all costs.

No matter what the story, the shtriga is a fascinating figure in Albanian folklore. It is a creature that is both feared and respected, and one that has been the subject of many tales and legends throughout the years. The shtriga is a creature that is deeply embedded in Albanian culture, and one that will continue to fascinate and intrigue people for years to come.

2.

A shtriga is a type of witch found in the folklore of Albania and other parts of the Mediterranean region. It is believed that these witches feed on the life force of infants and young children, draining them of their energy and causing them to become ill. As such, it is important to know how to kill a shtriga in order to protect the vulnerable and prevent them from suffering.

In order to kill a shtriga, one must first understand their nature and how they operate. Shtrigas are typically female, and they are said to be able to take the form of an owl, fly, or a human. They are also believed to possess the power of invisibility, allowing them to go undetected while they feed on their victims.

Once the shtriga has been identified, there are several methods that can be used to kill it. The most common way is to use a special type of iron, such as a nail or needle, to pierce the shtriga's heart. This must be done at night, as the shtriga is most vulnerable during this time. Additionally, the iron must be heated in a fire and blessed by a priest before it is used.

Another method for killing a shtriga is to use a special type of herb. This herb is believed to be able to weaken the shtriga and make it vulnerable to attack. It is important to note, however, that this herb must be gathered during a full moon and blessed by a priest.

Finally, it is believed that a shtriga can be killed by using a special type of incantation. This incantation must be spoken over the shtriga three times, and it must be spoken in a language that the shtriga does not understand. This incantation is believed to be able to break the shtriga's power and render it vulnerable to attack.

Killing a shtriga is no easy task, and it requires a great deal of knowledge and preparation. It is important to remember that these methods should only be used as a last resort, as the shtriga is a powerful creature and should not be taken lightly. Additionally, it is important to note that these methods may not always work, and there is no guarantee of success.

In conclusion, killing a shtriga is a difficult and dangerous task. It requires knowledge of the shtriga's nature and the proper methods for killing it. Additionally, it is important to keep in mind that these methods may not always work, and there is no guarantee of success. However, if the proper precautions are taken and the right methods are used, it is possible to rid oneself of this dangerous creature and protect the vulnerable from its evil.

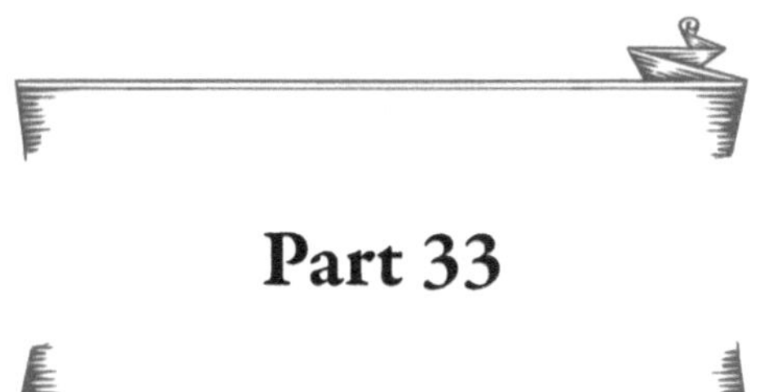

# Part 33

# Crocotta

# Crocotta
## 1.

A Crocotta is a mythical creature that has been featured in many different cultures throughout history. It is typically described as having the body of a wolf and the head of a crocodile. Depending on the region, it may also have the tail of a lion or the horns of a ram. The Crocotta is said to be a ferocious and powerful creature, with the strength and cunning of both a wolf and a crocodile.

The origin of the Crocotta is unclear, as it has been featured in many different cultures throughout history. It appears in ancient Egyptian and Greek mythology, as well as in various medieval European and Middle Eastern texts. In some cultures, the Crocotta is seen as a symbol of strength and courage, while in others it is seen as a harbinger of death and destruction.

In Greek mythology, the Crocotta is said to have been created by the gods to protect the city of Thebes from invaders. It is described as having the body of a wolf and the head of a crocodile, and it is said to have been so powerful that it could not be killed by any weapon. The Crocotta was said to be so fierce that it could even devour lions and bulls.

In some Middle Eastern cultures, the Crocotta is seen as a symbol of death and destruction. It is believed that when people die, their souls are transformed into Crocottas and sent to the underworld. In some cultures, the Crocotta is seen as a symbol of justice, as it is said to be able to detect and punish wrongdoers.

In medieval Europe, the Crocotta was believed to be a shape-shifting creature that could take on the form of a human or an animal. It was said to be able to manipulate people through fear and deception, and it was believed to be able to cause great harm and destruction. It was also believed to be able to cause disease and misfortune.

Today, the Crocotta is often seen as a symbol of strength and courage. It is a popular figure in fantasy literature and art, and it is often used as a symbol of power and protection. It is also seen as a symbol of justice, as it is said to be able to detect and punish wrongdoers.

In conclusion, the Crocotta is a mythical creature that has been featured in many different cultures throughout history. It is typically described as having the body of a wolf and the head of a crocodile, and it is said to be a ferocious and powerful creature. Depending on the region, it may also have the tail of a lion or the horns of a ram. In some cultures, it is seen as a symbol of strength and courage, while in others it is seen as a harbinger of death and destruction. It is a popular figure in fantasy literature and art, and it is often used as a symbol of power and protection.

2.

Killing a crocotta is no small feat. This mythical creature is described as a ferocious beast with the head of a wolf and the body of a hyena, making it a formidable opponent. For those brave enough to take on this challenge, there are a few steps to consider before making the attempt.

The first step to killing a crocotta is to understand its behavior. Crocottas are known to be incredibly aggressive and will attack anything that they perceive as a threat. It is important to remember that they are also incredibly fast and can move quickly over long distances. Additionally, they have a keen sense of smell and hearing, so it is essential to be aware of one's surroundings when hunting them.

Once the crocotta's behavior is understood, the next step is to prepare for the hunt. It is important to gather the necessary supplies, such as a bow and arrows, a spear, and a strong rope. These supplies will be necessary for the hunt, as the crocotta is a formidable opponent and will require a well-equipped hunter. Additionally, it is important to have a plan of attack, as the crocotta is a cunning creature and will be difficult to track and kill.

When the hunt is ready to begin, the next step is to locate the crocotta. This can be done by tracking its movements and looking for signs of its presence, such as footprints or droppings. Once the crocotta is located, the hunter must be extremely cautious and move slowly and silently. It is important to remember that the crocotta is incredibly fast and can move quickly over long distances, so the hunter must be prepared to act quickly when the opportunity arises.

Once the crocotta is located, the hunter can begin the attack. The most effective way to kill a crocotta is to use a bow and arrow, as this will allow the hunter to keep a safe distance from the creature. The hunter should aim for the crocotta's head or heart, as these are the most vulnerable spots. Additionally, a spear can be used to stab the crocotta, although this is a more dangerous approach and should only be used if the hunter is confident in their ability to hit the target.

Finally, once the crocotta is dead, the hunter must take care to dispose of the body. The best way to do this is to tie a strong rope around the crocotta's neck and drag it away from the area. This will ensure that no other creatures come into contact with the body and will also prevent any potential health risks to the hunter.

Killing a crocotta is no small feat and requires a great deal of preparation and caution. It is important to understand the creature's behavior and to have the necessary supplies before beginning the hunt. Once the crocotta is located, the hunter must be prepared to act quickly and accurately in order to bring down the creature. Finally, once the crocotta is dead, the hunter must take care to dispose of the body properly. With the right preparation and technique, it is possible to kill a crocotta and protect oneself from potential danger

# Part 34

# Banshee

# Banshee
## 1.

A banshee is a supernatural being from Irish folklore that is known to wail or scream when someone is about to die. The banshee is often associated with death and is said to be an omen of impending doom. In traditional Irish folklore, banshees are usually female figures, though some tales do mention male banshees.

The origin of the banshee is unclear, but some believe that it is a spirit of an ancestor who has returned to warn of an impending death. Others believe that the banshee is a spirit of the dead, or a spirit of the air. Whatever its origin, the banshee is a powerful figure in Irish folklore and its presence is often seen as a warning of death.

The banshee is said to take many forms, including a woman dressed in white, a hooded figure, an old woman, a fairy, and a crow. The banshee is said to be able to move through walls and is often seen near a house where a death is about to occur. The banshee is said to wail or scream, often in a shrill voice, to announce the impending death.

The banshee is often seen as a messenger of death, but it is also believed to be a protector as well. It is said that the banshee will stay with a family for generations, warning them of impending death and protecting them from harm. Many Irish families have stories of the banshee protecting them from danger, and some believe that the banshee is a guardian angel of sorts.

The banshee is a powerful figure in Irish folklore and its presence is often seen as a warning of death. It is believed to be a spirit of the dead, a messenger of death, and a protector of families. The banshee is a mysterious figure, shrouded in mystery and fear, but it is also a figure of comfort and protection to those who believe in its power.

The banshee is a powerful figure in Irish folklore and its presence is often seen as a warning of death. It is believed to be a spirit of the dead, a messenger of death, and a protector of families. It is a mysterious figure, shrouded in mystery and fear, but it is also a figure of comfort and protection to those who believe in its power. The banshee is a powerful symbol in Irish folklore and its presence is often seen as a sign of protection and safety.

2.

Killing a banshee is no easy task. A banshee is a mythical creature, typically associated with Celtic mythology, that is said to appear as a harbinger of death. The banshee is known to wail, shriek, or scream, often with a terrifyingly loud sound that can be heard from miles away. This sound is said to signify the impending death of someone close to the banshee. As such, many believe that killing a banshee is impossible.

However, there are several ways to kill a banshee. The most common way is to use a weapon, such as a sword or spear, to pierce the banshee's heart. This is said to be the only way to stop the banshee's wailing and end its life. Another way to kill a banshee is to use a magical spell or potion. This method is more difficult, as it requires knowledge of the correct spell or potion to use.

In addition to weapons and magic, some people believe that a banshee can be killed by certain herbs or plants. For example, some believe that burning a mixture of garlic, fennel, and rosemary can drive away a banshee. Others believe that planting a rowan tree near a house can ward off a banshee, as rowan trees are said to have protective powers.

Finally, some people believe that a banshee can be killed by simply ignoring it. This method requires a great deal of courage, as it is difficult to ignore the banshee's wailing and not be affected by it. However, if one can manage to ignore the banshee's cries, it is said that the banshee will eventually give up and leave, never to return.

Killing a banshee is not an easy task, and it should not be taken lightly. It is important to remember that the banshee is a mythical creature that is said to be a harbinger of death. As such, it should be treated with respect and caution. If one chooses to try and kill a banshee, they should use caution and research the appropriate methods for doing so. If done correctly, it is possible to kill a banshee and put an end to its wailing.

# Part 35

# Wraith

# Wraith
1.

Wraiths are powerful supernatural creatures that have been known to haunt and terrorize humans for centuries. They are known to be incredibly resilient and difficult to defeat, making them one of the most feared creatures in folklore. Despite their intimidating presence, there are several ways to effectively kill a wraith.

The first step in killing a wraith is to identify its weaknesses. Wraiths are vulnerable to certain elements and materials, such as iron, silver, and salt. Iron and silver can be used to create weapons that can be used to physically attack the wraith, while salt can be used to create a barrier that the wraith cannot cross. Additionally, some wraiths are vulnerable to holy symbols such as crosses and crucifixes. It is important to be aware of the wraith's weaknesses in order to effectively combat it.

Once the weaknesses of the wraith have been identified, the next step is to prepare for the battle. It is important to have a plan of attack and to gather any necessary materials beforehand. Creating weapons out of iron or silver, and gathering salt to create a barrier are important steps in the battle plan. Additionally, it is important to have a team of people to help in the battle. Having a group of people can help to distract the wraith and make it easier to attack.

Once the battle is ready to begin, the next step is to attack the wraith. Depending on the wraith's weaknesses, different weapons and tactics can be used. If the wraith is vulnerable to iron or silver, weapons made out of these materials can be used to physically attack the wraith. Additionally, holy symbols such as crosses and crucifixes can be used to weaken the wraith. Salt can also be used to create a barrier that the wraith cannot cross.

It is important to note that the battle with the wraith is likely to be long and difficult. Wraiths are incredibly resilient creatures and can take a considerable amount of damage before they are killed. Additionally, they are known to be incredibly powerful and can use their supernatural abilities to their advantage. It is important to be prepared for a long, difficult battle.

Killing a wraith is not an easy task, but it is possible. Identifying the wraith's weaknesses and preparing for the battle are important steps in the process. Once the battle begins, different weapons and tactics can be used to attack the wraith. It is important to remember that the battle is likely to be long and difficult, but with the right preparation and tactics, it is possible to kill a wraith.

2.

Killing a wraith is no easy task, and it requires a great deal of preparation and knowledge in order to be successful. A wraith is a supernatural creature that is said to haunt the living and bring them harm. They are known to be incredibly powerful and difficult to defeat, and as such, it takes a great deal of skill and courage to even attempt to take one down.

The first step to killing a wraith is to learn as much as you can about them. This includes researching their history, powers, and weaknesses. It is also important to understand their motivations and behavior so that you can anticipate their actions and be prepared for whatever they might throw at you. Knowing as much as possible about the wraith you are facing will give you the best chance of success.

Once you have done your research, the next step is to prepare yourself for battle. This includes gathering the necessary tools and weapons to fight the wraith. These can include things like holy water, silver weapons, and other items that are known to be effective against supernatural creatures. It is important to make sure that you are well-equipped and that you have a plan of attack before engaging the wraith.

When it comes to actually killing a wraith, there are several methods that can be used. The most common is to use a silver weapon to stab or slash the wraith. Silver is believed to be one of the few materials that can harm a wraith, and it is important to make sure that your weapon is sharp and strong enough to do the job. Additionally, you can use holy water to weaken the wraith and make it easier to defeat.

Another method of killing a wraith is to use a spell or ritual to banish it. This requires a great deal of knowledge and skill, as well as the correct materials and ingredients. The spell or ritual must be performed correctly and at the right time in order to be successful. It is also important to remember that the wraith may put up a fight and try to resist the ritual, so it is important to be prepared for this.

Finally, it is possible to trap a wraith in an object such as a mirror or a box. This requires a great deal of skill and preparation, as well as the right materials. The object must be crafted in a specific way in order to be able to contain the wraith, and it must be sealed shut in order to prevent the wraith from escaping.

Killing a wraith is no easy task, and it requires a great deal of preparation and knowledge in order to be successful. It is important to research the wraith you are facing and to make sure you are well-equipped with the necessary tools and weapons. Additionally, you must be prepared to use either a silver weapon, holy water, a spell or ritual, or a trapping object in order to be successful. With the right knowledge and preparation, it is possible to take down a wraith and protect yourself and those around you.

# Part 36

# Rakshasa

# R akshasa
## 1.

A rakshasa is a mythological creature in Hinduism and Buddhism. It is a powerful being that is often associated with chaos, destruction, and evil. Rakshasas are often depicted as having supernatural powers, such as shape-shifting and invisibility. They are also said to possess immense strength and cunning.

The origin of the rakshasa is unclear, but it is believed that they existed in Indian mythology as far back as the Vedic period. The earliest references to them can be found in the Rigveda, an ancient Hindu scripture. In the Rigveda, they are described as a powerful and destructive force that can cause chaos and destruction.

In Hindu mythology, the rakshasa is often portrayed as a demonic creature that is a threat to humans. It is said to have the power to possess humans and take over their bodies. In some stories, the rakshasa is said to be able to take on the form of a human or animal in order to deceive its victims.

Rakshasas are also said to possess magical powers, such as the ability to make themselves invisible or to transform into different creatures. They are often depicted as having an insatiable appetite for human flesh. In some stories, they are said to be able to create illusions and cast spells.

Rakshasas are often used in Hindu mythology as a symbol of evil and chaos. They are often portrayed as villains or antagonists in stories. They are also used to represent the forces of chaos and destruction that can threaten humanity.

In Buddhism, the rakshasa is seen as a powerful being that can cause suffering and disharmony. They are seen as a force of evil that must be defeated in order to achieve enlightenment. In some stories, the rakshasa is said to be a manifestation of the human ego and desires.

In some Hindu and Buddhist traditions, the rakshasa is believed to be a guardian of the underworld. It is said to protect the souls of the dead and keep them from entering the realm of the living.

The rakshasa is an important figure in Hindu and Buddhist mythology. It is a powerful and destructive force that can cause chaos and destruction. It is also seen as a symbol of evil and chaos, and is often used to represent the forces of darkness and destruction that can threaten humanity.

2.

Killing a rakshasa is no easy task, but it is possible. A rakshasa is a mythological creature that is considered to be an evil spirit in Hindu, Buddhist, and Jain mythology. They are often described as being powerful and dangerous creatures that can cause chaos and destruction. In order to successfully kill a rakshasa, one must be prepared with the right knowledge and tools.

The first step in killing a rakshasa is to understand their weaknesses. Rakshasas are said to be vulnerable to a variety of weapons, including swords, arrows, spears, and even fire. In addition, they are said to be vulnerable to the power of mantras and holy chants. These mantras and chants must be recited with great precision and power in order to be effective. It is also important to note that rakshasas are said to be repelled by the sight and smell of holy water, so it is important to have some on hand.

Once the proper weapons and holy chants have been gathered, it is time to prepare for battle. Rakshasas are said to be powerful and cunning, so it is important to be prepared for anything. It is important to have a plan of attack and to know the rakshasa's weaknesses. It is also important to be aware of any traps or tricks that the rakshasa may use to try to avoid being killed.

When the time comes to face the rakshasa, it is important to be brave and determined. The rakshasa may be powerful, but it is important to remember that it is still vulnerable to the weapons and holy chants that have been gathered. It is important to stay focused and to use the weapons and chants to their fullest potential.

Once the rakshasa has been defeated, it is important to ensure that it is completely dead. It is possible for a rakshasa to revive itself if it is not completely killed, so it is important to make sure that it is dead. This can be done by burning the body or by burying it in a deep grave.

Killing a rakshasa is no easy task, but it is possible. It is important to be prepared with the right knowledge and tools and to stay brave and determined in battle. It is also important to make sure that the rakshasa is completely dead in order to prevent it from coming back. With the right preparation and courage, it is possible to successfully kill a rakshasa.

# Part 37

# Laviathans

# Leviathans
### 1.

The concept of the Leviathan in the Bible is an interesting one, as it is referenced in several books of the Old Testament and is often used as a metaphor for powerful forces. In its simplest form, the Leviathan is a large sea creature, usually described as a serpent or a dragon, and is often seen as a symbol of chaos and destruction. This creature is mentioned in several books of the Bible, including Job, Psalms, Isaiah, and Amos. In each of these books, the Leviathan is used to represent something powerful and dangerous, and its presence is often seen as a warning or a reminder of the dangers of chaos and destruction.

The first reference to the Leviathan in the Bible is in the book of Job. In this book, God asks Job a series of questions about the Leviathan, and Job is unable to answer them. This is seen as a reminder of the power of God, and the fact that even the most powerful creatures are still subject to His will. This is further reinforced in the book of Psalms, where the Leviathan is referred to as "the King of all the earth" and is seen as a representation of God's power and authority.

In the book of Isaiah, the Leviathan is used to represent the chaos and destruction of war. The prophet Isaiah speaks of the Leviathan as a creature that is "piercing the deep" and is a symbol of the destruction that is caused by war. This is further reinforced in the book of Amos, where the Leviathan is used to represent the chaos and destruction caused by the Assyrian army.

The Leviathan is also mentioned in the book of Revelation, where it is used to represent the power of Satan. In this book, the Leviathan is described as a beast that has seven heads and ten horns, and is seen as a symbol of the power of evil. This is further reinforced in the book of Daniel, where the Leviathan is used to represent the power of the Antichrist.

The Leviathan is an interesting concept in the Bible, as it is used to represent a variety of powerful and dangerous concepts. It is seen as a reminder of the power of God, the chaos and destruction caused by war, and the power of evil. This creature is a powerful symbol that reminds us of the dangers of chaos and destruction, and the importance of submitting to the will of God.

2.

This mythical sea monster has been the subject of fascination for centuries, and tales of its immense size and strength have been passed down for generations. But, if one is brave enough to take on such a challenge, there are ways to go about it. Though it may seem impossible, it is possible to kill a leviathan with the right preparation and strategy.

The first step in killing a leviathan is to understand its anatomy and weaknesses. The leviathan is a large, serpentine creature with a thick hide and numerous tentacles. Its size and strength make it a formidable opponent, and its tentacles can be used to grapple and drag opponents. Additionally, its hide is highly resistant to most weapons, making it difficult to penetrate. To be successful, one must identify and exploit the leviathan's weaknesses.

One of the most common ways to kill a leviathan is to use a harpoon. Harpoons are large, barbed spears that can penetrate the leviathan's thick hide and cause massive damage. They can be thrown from a distance, making it easier to stay out of the leviathan's reach. Additionally, harpoons can be used to grapple and drag the leviathan to shore, making it easier to finish the job.

Another way to kill a leviathan is to use explosives. Explosives can be used to cause massive damage to the leviathan's hide, making it easier to penetrate. This method is often used in conjunction with harpoons, as the harpoons can be used to drag the leviathan closer to shore before the explosives are used.

Finally, one can use magical means to kill a leviathan. Magic can be used to weaken the leviathan, making it easier to kill. Spells such as levitation, fireballs, and lightning bolts can all be used to weaken the leviathan, making it easier to finish the job.

Killing a leviathan is no easy task, but it is possible with the right preparation and strategy. By understanding the leviathan's anatomy and weaknesses, one can use a combination of harpoons, explosives, and magic to bring it down. With enough courage and skill, one can successfully kill a leviathan and become a hero.

# Part 38

# Reapers

# Reapers

### 1.

The Reaper is described as a tall, skeletal figure, usually clad in a dark robe and hood. It is an entity of death, and its presence is often accompanied by a chill in the air and a sense of dread. It is an unstoppable force, and those who encounter it rarely survive. It is also known to be able to appear in a variety of forms, from a human to a black dog.

The Reaper is not an evil entity, however. It is a neutral force, and its job is to take the souls of the recently deceased to their final resting place. It is not responsible for deciding who lives and who dies, and it is not responsible for the fate of those it takes. It is simply an agent of death, and its presence is often seen as a sign that someone's time has come.

The Reaper is also known to have a powerful connection to the supernatural world. It can sense when a creature of the supernatural is nearby, and it is often the first to arrive when a supernatural creature is slain. It is also known to take the souls of creatures of the supernatural, such as angels and demons, and it is often called upon by powerful figures in the supernatural world to take the souls of those they wish to be rid of.

### 2.

A reaper is a supernatural entity that is responsible for collecting the souls of the dead and guiding them to the afterlife. They are powerful beings, so it takes a great deal of strength and knowledge to take one down. The most effective way to kill a reaper is to use a weapon that has been imbued with powerful magical properties.

There are several different weapons that can be used to kill a reaper. The most common weapon is a sword that has been imbued with powerful magical properties. This type of sword can be found in many different places, including ancient ruins and tombs. Additionally, some powerful wizards can create a special sword that has the power to kill a reaper.

Another weapon that can be used to kill a reaper is an enchanted arrow. These arrows can be created by powerful wizards and imbued with powerful magical properties. They are able to penetrate the reaper's armor and slay them. Additionally, some powerful wizards can create a special arrow that has the power to kill a reaper.

In addition to weapons, powerful spells can be used to kill a reaper. These spells must be cast by powerful wizards who have a great deal of knowledge and experience in the magical arts. Some of the more powerful spells are known as death curses, which are able to instantly slay a reaper. Additionally, some powerful wizards can create a special spell that has the power to kill a reaper.

Finally, some powerful wizards can create a magical artifact that has the power to kill a reaper. These artifacts are extremely powerful and can be found in ancient ruins and tombs. Additionally, some powerful wizards can create a special artifact that has the power to kill a reaper.

No matter what weapon or spell is used to kill a reaper, it is important to remember that it takes a great deal of strength and knowledge to take one down. Additionally, it is important to remember that reapers are powerful supernatural entities and should not be taken lightly. If one is not prepared for the task of killing a reaper, it is best to leave it to the experts.

# Part 39

# Khan Worm

# Khan Worm
### 1.

It is an ancient, parasitic creature that feeds on the life force of its hosts, leaving them weakened and vulnerable. The Khan Worm has been around since the dawn of time, and it is believed to be the source of many of the world's supernatural occurrences.

The Khan Worm is a powerful creature that can possess humans and animals alike, and it can even take control of its host's mind. It is capable of manipulating its victims, making them do its bidding and allowing it to feed on their life force. It is also capable of creating illusions and manipulating reality, making it a formidable opponent for any hunter.

The Khan Worm is an ancient creature, and it has been around since the dawn of time. It is believed to be the source of many of the world's supernatural occurrences, such as hauntings, curses, and other paranormal events. It is also believed to be the cause of many illnesses and diseases, as it feeds on the life force of its victims and can weaken them.

The Khan Worm is a creature of immense power, and it is feared by many hunters. It is capable of possessing its victims and controlling their minds, as well as creating illusions and manipulating reality. It is a formidable opponent, and it is not something to be taken lightly.

The Khan Worm is a powerful creature that is feared by many hunters. It is an ancient creature, and it has been around since the dawn of time. It is capable of possessing humans and animals alike, as well as creating illusions and manipulating reality. It is a formidable opponent, and it is not something to be taken lightly. It is believed to be the source of many of the world's supernatural occurrences, and it is capable of weakening its victims and feeding on their life force. The Khan Worm is a powerful creature, and it should be respected and feared by all hunters.

2.

Killing the supernatural Khan Worm can be a daunting task, as it is a creature of legend and myth. It is said to be a giant, carnivorous worm that can grow up to a hundred feet long and is said to inhabit the dark places of the world. Despite its mysterious origins, there are ways to kill the Khan Worm, and it is important to understand them in order to protect yourself and others from this dangerous creature.

The first step to killing the Khan Worm is to determine its exact location. This can be difficult, as it is said to inhabit the darkest and most remote places on the planet. However, it is possible to track the Khan Worm by listening for its distinctive call, which is said to sound like a low-pitched growl. Once located, the next step is to prepare for battle.

When engaging the Khan Worm, it is important to be aware of its formidable strength and size. It is said to possess an incredibly thick hide that is almost impenetrable, so it is important to have a weapon that is capable of penetrating its armor. The most effective weapons against the Khan Worm are magical in nature, such as enchanted swords or spears. It is also important to bring a large number of allies, as the Khan Worm is known to be a formidable opponent even when outnumbered.

Once the Khan Worm is engaged, it is important to be prepared for a long and difficult battle. The creature is said to possess a variety of powerful magical abilities that can be used to protect itself and attack its opponents. It is also said to possess an incredible regenerative ability, which means that it can heal itself even when severely injured. In order to defeat the Khan Worm, it is important to wear it down over time and to be prepared for a long and arduous fight.

The final step to killing the Khan Worm is to use a powerful magical item known as the Sword of the Khan. This magical blade is said to be the only weapon capable of piercing the Khan Worm's thick hide and delivering a fatal blow. However, the Sword of the Khan is said to be incredibly difficult to obtain, as it is said to be hidden away in a secret location.

Killing the Khan Worm is a difficult and dangerous task, but it is possible with the right preparation and knowledge. It is important to be aware of its formidable strength and magical abilities, and to be prepared for a long and difficult battle. Additionally, it is important to obtain the Sword of the Khan in order to deliver a fatal blow to the creature. With the right preparation and knowledge, the Khan Worm can be defeated and the world can be made safer.

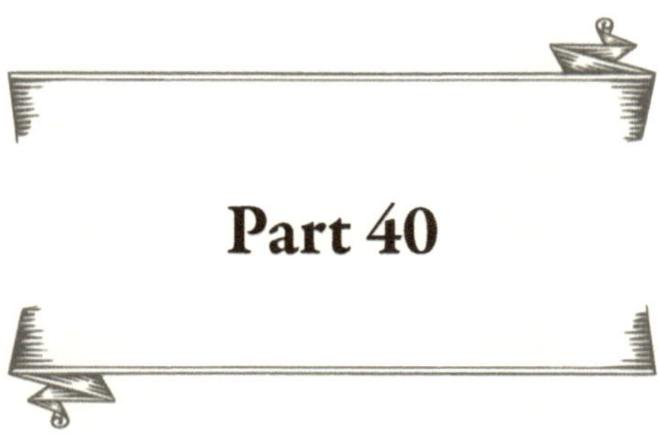

# Part 40

# ghosts

# Ghost
### 1.

A ghost is a supernatural phenomenon that has been reported throughout history in various cultures and societies. It is typically characterized as an apparition or entity that appears in a physical form, usually resembling a human or animal, and is often said to be the spirit of a deceased person. The term "ghost" is derived from the Old English word "gast", which means "breath" or "soul".

The concept of ghosts has been around for centuries and is deeply ingrained in many cultures and religions. Ancient Egyptians believed in the afterlife and the idea of a spirit that could remain after the death of the body. In some cultures, there is a belief that the spirit of the dead can remain on Earth in order to protect or watch over their loved ones. In other cultures, there is a belief that ghosts are the souls of those who have died but have yet to ascend to the afterlife.

The exact nature of ghosts is still a matter of debate. Some believe that ghosts are the result of supernatural forces, while others believe that they are a manifestation of the human psyche. It is also possible that ghosts are a combination of both, and that they are a product of both the physical and spiritual realms.

While there is no scientific evidence to prove the existence of ghosts, there have been countless reports of sightings and encounters with them throughout history. In many cases, people have reported feeling a presence in a room, hearing disembodied voices, or seeing unexplained phenomena such as objects moving on their own. In some cases, people have reported feeling a cold chill or feeling a presence in the room, or even seeing the ghost itself.

Theories about ghosts vary widely, and there is no single accepted explanation for their existence. Some believe that ghosts are the spirits of the dead, while others believe that they are the result of psychological phenomena. Some believe that ghosts are the result of paranormal activity or hauntings, while others believe that they are the result of energy fields or spiritual entities.

Whatever the cause, it is clear that ghosts have been a part of human culture for centuries. They can be seen as a reminder of our mortality, a source of comfort in times of grief, or a source of fear and mystery. Whether or not ghosts actually exist, they remain a fascinating topic of discussion and debate.

2.

Ghosts have been a source of fascination for centuries, and many cultures have their own ways of interacting with them. For some, the idea of a ghost is a comforting one, while for others, it can be a source of fear and dread. But what if you want to get rid of a ghost that is causing trouble? How do you go about killing or destroying a ghost?

The first thing to remember is that ghosts are not physical beings, so the idea of killing them in the traditional sense is impossible. However, there are several ways to get rid of a ghost that don't involve violence. The most common method is to use religious symbols or prayers to drive the ghost away. This is a popular practice in many cultures, and is often used to drive away evil spirits or ghosts. Some people also believe that burning certain plants or herbs can help to ward off ghosts.

Another method of getting rid of a ghost is to use a magical ritual. This can involve burning certain items, such as candles, incense, or herbs, or it can involve the use of symbols or words of power. This type of ritual is often used to banish ghosts or other supernatural entities from a particular area.

In some cases, it may be necessary to perform an exorcism in order to get rid of a ghost. This is a complex ritual that is often performed by a priest or other religious figure. It involves reciting specific prayers or words of power in order to drive the ghost away. This type of ritual is often used in cases where a ghost is causing physical harm, or is otherwise terrorizing a person or group of people.

Finally, if all else fails, it may be necessary to call upon a powerful spirit or deity to help get rid of a ghost. This is a more extreme measure and should only be done in cases where the ghost is causing serious harm or disruption. The spirit or deity can then be called upon to banish the ghost from the area.

In conclusion, it is possible to get rid of a ghost without resorting to violence. Religious symbols or prayers, magical rituals, exorcisms, and calling upon powerful spirits or deities are all methods that can be used to get rid of a ghost. However, it is important to remember that each situation is unique, and the best course of action will depend on the particular circumstances.

# Conclusion.

**Spells**

The idea of monsters lurking in the shadows can be a scary thought for many people. Fortunately, there is a way to get rid of them: a good spell. While there are many different spells that can be used to ward off monsters, some are more effective than others. This essay will explore what makes a good spell to get rid of monsters and how to cast it.

When it comes to casting a spell to get rid of monsters, it's important to remember that the power of the spell lies in its intention. The spell must be cast with a clear purpose in mind: to drive away the monsters. It is also important to use words that are powerful and meaningful, as this will help to make the spell more effective. For example, you may want to use words such as "banish" or "expel" to emphasize the power of the spell.

When it comes to the ingredients used to cast the spell, it is important to choose those that are associated with protection. Herbs such as lavender, rosemary, and thyme are often used in spells to ward off monsters, as they are believed to have protective properties. Additionally, it is important to use the right type of candle for the spell. White candles are often used in spells to get rid of monsters, as they are believed to be a powerful symbol of protection.

The next step in casting a spell to get rid of monsters is to choose the right time to cast it. It is believed that the time of day or night can have an effect on the power of the spell. For example, it is believed that the best time to cast a spell is during a waning moon, as this is when the energy of the moon is decreasing. Additionally, it is important to choose a time when you are feeling focused and clear-minded, as this will help to make the spell more effective.

Finally, it is important to remember that a spell is only as effective as the person casting it. In order for the spell to be successful, the caster must be confident and believe in the power of the spell. It is also important to be mindful of the words used, as they will help to give the spell more power.

In conclusion, a good spell to get rid of monsters must be cast with a clear intention, use powerful words, and be cast at the right time. Additionally, the caster must have faith in the power of the spell and use ingredients that are associated with protection. With these components in place, a good spell to get rid of monsters can be successful.

**Lores**

The concept of lores that can kill monsters is an intriguing one, as it implies the existence of powerful forces that can be used to battle and defeat creatures of the unknown. In the world of fantasy and adventure, lores are often used to describe special abilities, spells or weapons that can be employed to vanquish monsters and other creatures of the night. But what exactly are these lores, and how can they be used to achieve victory?

To answer this question, it is important to first understand what lores are. In its simplest form, lores are stories, tales, or myths that have been passed down through generations, often with the purpose of imparting wisdom or knowledge. They can also be used to describe powerful magical abilities or weapons that can be used to fight off monsters. In the world of fantasy and adventure, lores can be used to describe powerful magical abilities, spells, and weapons that can be used to fight off monsters and other creatures of the night.

One of the most common lores used to kill monsters is the use of magical weapons. In many fantasy stories, heroes are equipped with magical swords, bows, and other weapons that can be used to vanquish their foes. These weapons are often imbued with powerful enchantments that make them especially effective against monsters. For example, in the Lord of the Rings trilogy, the hero Aragorn wields a magical sword called Anduril, which is able to cut through the toughest of monsters.

Another common lore used to kill monsters is the use of powerful spells and incantations. In many fantasy stories, heroes are able to cast spells and recite incantations that can be used to vanquish their foes. For example, in the Harry Potter series, Harry and his friends are able to use powerful spells such as the Expelliarmus charm to disarm their enemies and the Patronus Charm to ward off dark creatures. The power of these spells and incantations can be used to defeat even the most powerful of monsters.

Finally, lores can also be used to describe powerful magical artifacts that can be used to vanquish monsters. In many fantasy stories, heroes are able to wield powerful artifacts such as the Sword of Gryffindor from the Harry Potter series or the One Ring from the Lord of the Rings trilogy. These artifacts are often imbued with powerful enchantments that make them especially effective against monsters.

In conclusion, lores can be used to describe powerful magical abilities, spells, weapons, and artifacts that can be used to vanquish monsters. These lores can be found in many different forms, from magical weapons to powerful spells and incantations, and even powerful artifacts. By understanding the power of these lores, heroes can use them to their advantage in order to defeat even the most powerful of monsters.

## WEAPONS

When it comes to killing monsters, there are many different weapons that can be used to accomplish this feat. Whether you're a novice or an experienced monster hunter, it's important to pick the right weapon for the job. While there is no one-size-fits-all solution, there are some weapons that are better suited for taking down monsters than others.

The first weapon that comes to mind is a sword. Swords are a classic weapon that have been used for centuries to slay monsters. They offer a wide variety of advantages, such as being lightweight and easy to wield, while also providing good reach and power. Swords are also versatile, allowing you to choose between a variety of styles and materials, such as steel or titanium.

Another weapon that can be used to kill monsters is a bow and arrow. Bows and arrows are a great choice for hunters who want to keep their distance from their targets. They offer excellent accuracy and power, and can be used to take down even the toughest of monsters. Bows and arrows also offer the added benefit of being relatively quiet, making them a great choice for stealthy hunters.

If you're looking for something a bit more powerful, then you might want to consider a gun. Guns are great for taking down monsters from a distance, and they can be loaded with a variety of ammunition types, such as bullets, shells, and even explosive rounds. While guns can be loud, they can also be silenced, making them ideal for stealthy hunters.

Finally, there are magical weapons. These weapons often come in the form of wands, staffs, and other items that contain powerful enchantments. They are often used by experienced monster hunters, as they can be used to cast powerful spells and enchantments that can take down even the toughest of monsters.

No matter which weapon you choose, it's important to remember that each weapon has its own advantages and disadvantages. It's important to take the time to research and compare different weapons before making a decision. Additionally, it's important to practice with the weapon of your choice to ensure that you are comfortable and confident in using it. With the right weapon and a bit of practice, you'll be ready to take on any monster.

Did you love *The Hunter's Guide to Monsters*? Then you should read *The Witch Essay*[1] by EB Robichaud!

[2]

The Witch Essay is a series of essays that I have generated about the different kinds of witches and magic. each section has three essays.

---

1. https://books2read.com/u/b5wkLw

2. https://books2read.com/u/b5wkLw

# Also by EB Robichaud

**Kin of the Hunted**

Kin of the Hunted

Joel, the vampire


**Standalone**

Escaping Cold Lake

Escaping Cold Lake

The Witch Essay

The Hunter's Guide to Monsters

# About the Author

EB Robichaud was born in Eastern Canada and now resides in Alberta with his family